Beach Break

Debby Fowler

A Felicity Paradise crime novel

ISBN 978 185022 231 6

Published by Truran, Goonance, Water Lane,
St Agnes, Cornwall TR5 0RA
www.truranbooks.co.uk

Truran is an imprint of Truran Books Ltd

www.felicityparadise.com

Acknowledgements
I would particularly like to thank all in the
St Ives Harbour office, Dr Lucy Macfarlane,
Jo Pearce, Heather & Ivan Corbett and Kate Richards

Printed and bound in Cornwall by R. Booth Ltd,
The Praze, Penryn, TR10 8AA

This one is for you Jo with grateful thanks
for all your help

PROLOGUE

July 1989, The City of London

By the time he had finished speaking, the air in the boardroom was crackling with tension. Hugh Randall studied the five men before him. Only minutes ago they had spread themselves around the long boardroom table exchanging pleasantries, brimming with confidence, enthusiasm and good humour – and well they might for they were five of the most ambitious and experienced merchant bankers in the country – in the financial world, come to that. Now, however, they looked both alert and alarmed – billions of pounds were at stake and money was their lifeblood.

Jeremy Silversmith was the first to recover his composure, which was not surprising. He was well known for his ability to tease out problems, shaking them like a terrier with a rat until a solution was found.

'So what you are saying, Hugh, is that we've

bought the Carlyon Bank on the grounds of its not insubstantial assets only to find that one of those assets is a rogue trader?'

'Alex Button is no rogue trader,' said Hugh firmly, 'and he certainly hasn't been investing the Bank's money for his own gain, he has simply been dealing in futures in a very inappropriate and foolhardy manner. On paper it appears he has made millions for the Bank but many, well to be frank, most of the investments he has made are on the wild side and extremely high risk. Nothing detracts from the fact that we have acquired one of the oldest and most well-established banks in the world, with an excellent reputation for fair and honourable trading and a most impressive balance sheet. It's just that I thought you should know all is not quite what it seems.'

Jeremy was clearly unimpressed, 'So how it is we have only just stumbled across the activities of this Button fellow?'

'Poor management,' Hugh said. 'He was left entirely to his own devices. I gather he operated from a broom cupboard on the fifth floor and the Board were clearly delighted with his results without taking the trouble to see how he was managing to achieve them.'

'I trust he's been sacked?' roared Adam Dakin. Overweight and crimson of complexion at the best of times, he was now a dangerous shade of purple.

'That's why I wanted to talk to you,' said Hugh,

patiently. 'I think it would be very foolhardy indeed to sack Alex Button at the moment.'

'But if we know he's been gambling with Bank money inappropriately ...' Jeremy Silversmith began.

Hugh interrupted him. 'If we sack him he will go straight to the press. He has nothing to lose and if he did go public, we'd be finished.'

There was a silence around the boardroom table.

'Not necessarily,' Adam began.

'Without a shadow of doubt,' Hugh Randall thundered. 'We know that the banking business is all about confidence. If it becomes public knowledge that we've bought a pig in a poke, not only will Carlyon be finished but so will we – our reputations, and everything we've built up both jointly and severally over the years.'

'Because one chinless wonder in a broom cupboard says so?' Adam bellowed back. 'I'd have thought our collective reputations somewhat eclipse his.' There were vigorous nods around the boardroom table.

Hugh sighed. Intellectually these men had to be amongst the top one per cent in the world and yet they seemed to have a collective blind spot as to the dangers of the situation. 'We can't sack him,' Hugh repeated, 'but I do have a solution.'

'Which is?' Jeremy asked.

'Send him to Hong Kong.' Hugh replied, 'It's Carlyon's smallest branch and the Chairman out there is a good chap – Tony Wong, some of you may know him?'

There were a few grunts of acknowledgement.

'Tony's brief will be to keep a very tight rein on Button, clearly the chap's not without talent. However, if things don't work out and we have to let him go, by then Carlyon will be flourishing under our ownership. If at that stage, Button did go to the press he would be seen just as some whinging incompetent. It's right now that he's dangerous.'

'And what if he doesn't accept the post in Hong Kong?' Jeremy asked.

Hugh smiled slightly. 'He already has.'

1

August 2008, St Ives, Cornwall

Chief Inspector Keith Penrose was in a vile mood. He was both miserable and angry and the anger was directed at himself. He was acutely aware that he had spent a fruitless morning wasting both taxpayers' money and his own time. There had been nothing much going on at the station – the piles of paperwork on his desk depressed him and it was a beautiful day. There was a new and valuable exhibition opening at the Tate Gallery and he had convinced himself that it would be a good idea to visit St Ives and make a courtesy call to Security, just to see that all was well. It was a very lame excuse and he knew it.

As anticipated, the meeting at the Tate had been brief, pointless and faintly bewildering to the staff. Preceding that he had spent an hour sitting in traffic jams, both on the Hayle bypass and on the route through Carbis Bay into St Ives. By the time he walked down the steps from the Tate, the sun was high and the pavements choked with visitors. Porthmeor Beach had been turned into tent city, there was hardly a spare piece of sand to be seen. Briefly he looked across the road to the Porthmeor Beach Café but already it appeared to be full. He turned right and within a couple of minutes he plunged into the familiar streets which led down to the harbour … then he was there – at his true destination, not the Tate Gallery at all but Jericho Cottage, the home of Felicity Paradise.

He paused outside her eccentrically-painted purple door and smiled at it inanely, as if it was a friend. He knew she wasn't there, he knew she was in Oxford and would be remaining there until September but still he had hoped, vainly he knew, that she had come home early, that she missed Cornwall, perhaps even missed him. He glanced upwards – the French windows which led onto her little balcony were firmly shut, something they would never be if the owner was in residence. A fresh air freak, she rarely closed them and certainly not on a morning like this. He sighed and continued on his way towards the harbour. By the time he reached the Sloop Inn, the crowds were thicker still. He had intended to buy a sandwich and a coffee at the pub, but on fighting his way to the bar, he saw that waiting for food was hopeless. Instead he ordered a small glass of red wine and took it outside. There was room for one on the end of a table; he sat down and sipped his wine. The tide was in, the sun sparkling on the water; the harbour was crowded with boats of all sizes and shapes. The world promenaded past him and he watched it idly – buggies, dogs, wet sandy children, street traders pushing their barrows, surf boards, wet suits, ice creams, pasties, laughter, quarrels – all of life was here.

He was conscious suddenly of one or two people glancing in his direction and realized how conspicuous he must look in his jacket and tie; he was hot and uncomfortable too. What was he doing here anyway? He drained his wine glass and stood up. Heading along the harbour he stopped at a pasty shop, bought a pasty and a bottle of water and continued on to Smeaton's Pier where, at last, the crowds seemed to thin. He walked to the end of the pier, almost to the lighthouse and after finding a bench facing the sun sat down with some relief. There were a few children pier-jumping but apart from them he was on his own. He discreetly ate his pasty aware that a thousand seagull eyes would be on him, drank his water and then removed his tie and jacket. He leaned back on the bench and shut his eyes.

He had no good reason for this black cloud of melancholy which seemed to be sitting on his shoulders. Things were good at home, better than they had been for a long time. His wife Barbara was very involved at work and loving it. The various District Councils across Cornwall were being amalgamated into one single Cornwall Council. As a senior member of the Planning Committee of Carrick District Council, Barbara was up to her eyes in reorganisation plans. There was meeting after meeting and she was in her element. Carly, his daughter, was good too. After the terrifying year in which she had battled with Hodgkin's Lymphoma, she seemed to be in permanent remission. She had finished her training as a physiotherapist and was now working up in Plymouth with a flat of her own and a new and pleasant enough boyfriend who worked as a marine biologist at the University. Recognising that there was no man on earth who would be good enough for his daughter, Keith had to admit that Carly's Graham seemed a fairly nice chap. Will, his son, was coming good, too. After a bad experience in the Army in Afghanistan, followed by a dishonourable discharge and a serious personal crisis, Will seemed to be straightening out. The Falmouth boatbuilding course he had enrolled upon was going well and in the holidays he was working as a waiter in a restaurant in Truro. Keith knew how hard it was for Will after the responsibilities of Army life suddenly to be back to being a student and living at home. There had been rows and upsets and Will's drinking was still not fully under control but he was better, much better and calmer. If he still had not come to terms with the horrors he had witnessed – which Keith was sure he had not – at least they appeared no longer to dominate his life.

After a long and successful career in the police force, Keith was now only a few years off retirement. He knew he was exceptionally fit for his age, loved his work and enjoyed the company of his colleagues. He had every reason to feel buoyant and optimistic about the future and yet thoughts of Felicity Paradise dominated his waking hours. Why had she suddenly gone haring off to Oxford like that? Was she planning to leave Cornwall for good, had he driven her away with the awkwardness of their situation? Was she perhaps bored, lonely? Surely with her daughter down here and her granddaughter, she was settled. Normally he understood her, knew what she was thinking, but the brief telephone call in which she had told him she was going back up to Oxford for six weeks during the height of the season had left him confused, miserable and with the odd sense of being abandoned. It was ridiculous, of course. They were friends and nothing more, never could be. He was married, she was a widow and needed to find someone with whom she could share her life, for she was too young to be alone. He was not being fair. He knew she cared about him deeply but putting some distance between them surely was not such a bad thing in the circumstances. So why did he feel so absurdly hurt?

August 2008, Oxford

At the same moment that Keith Penrose was brooding on the pier, the object of his thoughts was also sunk in gloom. Felicity Paradise was sitting morosely in a café in the covered market in Oxford. It was a beautiful day but the café was hot and steamy, the grey lukewarm tasteless stuff she was drinking bore no relationship at all, as far as she could see, to a cup of coffee. She was missing her daughter, her granddaughter, she was missing the sea and her home and yes, she was missing Keith Penrose.

'In Cornwall dogs are always allowed in the cafés and bars, even restaurants sometimes,' Felicity grumbled at her best friend Gilla who was sitting opposite her.

'Fizzy, that's absolute rubbish and you know it,' Gilla responded with some spirit. 'I'm fed up with your moaning, I really am. I was so looking forward to you coming to Oxford and ever since you've arrived, you've done nothing but moan and groan and talk about Cornwall. If you're missing Cornwall so much why don't you go back there?' Her wonderful green eyes flashed dangerously.

'I'm sorry, I'm so sorry,' Felicity's remorse was genuine. 'I'm just something of a mess at the moment.' Tears crowded into her eyes; she rubbed them away with her fist like a child.

'Oh, Fizzy, for God's sake why didn't you say something was wrong? Come on, this coffee is dreadful, you're right. Let's go and find a glass of wine and then you can tell me what's really going on.'

Ten minutes later they were in the garden of a wine bar in Little Clarendon Street.

'I probably could have brought Harvey here,' Felicity said, referring to her Jack Russell terrier left forlornly behind in Gilla's house.

'Oh Fizzy, do shut up about that dog,' said Gilla, who was no animal lover. 'Just tell me why you're in such a state.'

'I can't,' Felicity replied after a moment, 'it would be a betrayal of trust.'

'Fizzy, I'm getting seriously fed up now,' said Gilla. 'We have been friends virtually all our lives. Do you really think there is anything that you could tell me which I'm not capable of keeping to myself, if that's what you want? It's so insulting!' She leant across and took one of Felicity's hands in hers. 'We've been through so much together, darling; surely to God if something is worrying you, you can tell me?'

'I ran away from Cornwall because of a man.' Felicity blurted out at last.

'A man?' said Gilly, clearly delighted. 'Fantastic, and about time, too.' Then seeing Felicity's expression she sobered. 'Sorry, sorry, clearly he's a bastard to have upset you but I'm just so pleased you've shown an interest in somebody, it's been too long, it really has.'

'You can't judge everyone by your own standards,' Felicity bit back, uncharacteristically vicious. The shock of her words silenced them both. 'I'm sorry,' Felicity said at last, 'I have absolutely no right to take this out on you, you of all people. You're quite right, you are my best friend, someone who is taking the time and trouble to listen to my woes and all I can do is …'

'OK, OK, apology accepted, now spill the beans Fizzy, or I'm walking right out of here.'

'It's Keith Penrose,' Felicity said after a moment.

'Your policeman, I knew it, I knew there was something going on there. He's married isn't he? So you're having an affair? What fun!'

'No we're not and it's not,' said Felicity, firmly.

'He doesn't care about you then, the man must be mad.'

'No, no,' said Felicity, miserably. 'He does care about me, rather a lot I think.'

'So what are you waiting for, darling, go get him.'

Felicity shook her head, studying her friend in silence for a moment. Gilla still looked so young for her age, her bright red curls showed no sign of grey, there was hardly a line on her skin and her figure was that of a girl. There had always been a man in Gilla's life, currently it was her long-suffering husband Simon, to whom in the last couple of years she had become reunited after years apart. Felicity hoped so much their relationship would last but fidelity was not one of Gilla's strong points.

'Look,' she said, 'what I said just now about you was harsh and rude and I apologise, but there is some truth in it. The thing is that I love Keith and Keith loves me but he is married, so married. He doesn't want to be unfaithful to his wife and I don't want him to be – neither of us could be happy at the expense of someone else's unhappiness. It may sound too facile; it may sound pious, pathetic and unadventurous, but that's how we feel, both of us.'

Gilla looked suitably contrite. She took Felicity's hand again. 'I'm sorry too and I promise what you say I am taking seriously,' she said. 'In fact I admire you, both you and your policeman for your principles but I think you're utterly deluded. As far as we know, we only get one crack at this life. Here you have a man who you love and who loves you. He wouldn't be in love with you if his marriage was satisfactory. If you can have some fun and bring each other some comfort and joy, take it Fizzy, darling, for God's sake.'

'There is another thing,' Felicity said, ignoring her.

'Which is?' Gilla smirked. 'At least I know it isn't that you're pregnant, there are some advantages of old age.'

Felicity smiled back. 'No, it's certainly not that.'
'What then?'

13

'After you, he is my best friend,' she said. 'I have settled very well in Cornwall but I don't know what I would have done without his friendship, companionship, call it what you like. He is always there for me. If we had an affair it could destroy that and his friendship is far more important to me than love or sex or whatever you want to apply to our relationship. In a strange sort of way, although he has a wife and a family at home and plenty of colleagues at work, I think I fulfil the same role, the same need in him. He knows I will always be there for him. So quite apart from the morals of the situation there is too much at stake, too much to lose.'

'So,' said Gilla, doing sign language at a waiter for him to top up their glasses. 'If that is the case, why are you here in Oxford all miserable and biting my head off?'

'As I explained to you on the phone I'm tired and need a break,' Felicity said. 'Mel has stopped work now and is expecting the new baby in five weeks time so she doesn't really need me babysitting. She's breezed through this pregnancy and she will want help once the new one is born, so it was a good opportunity for me to get away.' She hesitated. 'And August in St Ives is always gruesome, so many visitors, hard to get about ...'

'All very commendable, practical reasons,' Gilla interrupted, 'but it doesn't quite stack up. What are you leaving out?'

'You don't give up easily, do you?' said Felicity with a smile.

'No, I don't,' Gilla agreed.

'Well,' said Felicity, 'I think my relationship with Keith was starting to make me feel more miserable than happy.'

'Why?' Gilla demanded.

'We arrange to meet and I am so happy and excited at the prospect of seeing him and then we have a lovely time, lunch or occasionally an evening drink, and then an hour or so later, we part and I feel so let down and empty, somehow. He goes back to his family, I go back to Harvey and my lovely cottage but it's the emotional swings that I find so wearing; so happy one moment, lost and lonely the next. I wish our relationship was like it was in the beginning but we've said too many things now, made too many commitments as to how we feel, and they just can't be unsaid.'

'You've really got it bad, haven't you?' said Gilla.

Felicity nodded. 'And I can't think why, he couldn't be more different from Charlie.'

'What is he like?' Gilla asked, clearly intrigued.

'Well, physically he is very different from Charlie – he's dark where Charlie was fair, shorter and a lot fitter, although that wouldn't be hard. Poor Charlie did so love his lunches out and dinners in college.'

'I'm not asking you to compare him to your sadly deceased husband. I'm asking you to tell me what he's actually like,' said Gilla, clearly exasperated.

'Kind,' said Felicity, 'funny, we laugh a lot. We like the same things – dogs, children, wine, beautiful views – we even have the same taste in music.'

'This sounds absolutely deadly, darling, don't you have anything to argue about? What does he think, for example, of your little moments, does he even know about them?'

'Yes, he does know about them, and he certainly didn't believe in them at first,' said Felicity. 'It wasn't personal, it's just he didn't believe in such things as second sight. However it's got to a point now where he does actually ask me to become involved in the odd case if he's stuck – and I have come up with some results. So now he has to recognise my funny turns for what they are and I think he values them. He's not an intellectual like Charlie,' Fizzy continued, warming to her theme. 'Charlie was too clever for me really, but Keith is a clever man in a different way, more comfortable somehow.'

'What would Charlie think of him if he was still alive?' Gilla asked.

'They would get on alright, I suppose. After all, law is the common denominator – Charlie a lawyer, Keith a policeman. I just feel safe with Keith in a way I never did with Charlie, I was always trying to keep up with him.'

'That's ridiculous, Fizzy. You provided him with a lovely home and two children; he'd have been lost without you.'

'But we were very different people and liked doing different things, he was such a snob, dear old Charlie – our friends had nothing in common, we didn't share the same interests. When he died, I was devastated, as you know, but I have felt more myself in the last few years than I've done since I was a girl, since before I was married. Keith hasn't changed that, I don't have to be anything or anyone but me when I'm with Keith, it's more relaxing I suppose.'

'So what are you going to do?' Gilla asked.

'Nothing,' said Felicity, firmly. 'Let's have some lunch while we're here and let's chat about you and Simon and I promise to stop moping. If I may I'll stay with you for another few days and then I'll go home.'

'I thought you were here for a month?' Gilla said.

'I was, but I think I should go back and learn to live with the situation. Now I've shared this with someone, well not someone, with you, my dear best chum, I feel a whole lot better. It'll be alright. Thank you, Gilla, what would I do without you?'

'But you can't just leave things as they are, what are you going to do, Fizzy?' Gilla persisted.

'Nothing,' said Felicity, 'there's nothing to do, just learn to live with it.'

'First you pine for your dead husband and then you pine for someone who is not available. Time marches on darling, you need someone in your life, someone to share it with.'

17

'I have,' said Felicity. 'I have Harvey.'
'That bloody little mutt,' Gilla said.

2

Tonight was Felicity's last in Oxford and was by far the most pleasant. During the remainder of her stay which had lasted only ten days, it felt as if Gilla had invited just about every single male of a certain age in Oxford to share dinner with them in an attempt to distract Felicity from whom she still described as 'your policeman'. Among the rogues gallery had been a deeply boring banker friend of Simon's, a solicitor who had known and clearly admired Charlie and wouldn't stop regaling them with minutiae of every case they had worked on together and, to top it all, a salesman who supplied much of the tat Gilla sold in her Woodstock shop who was the epitome of a salesman – smarmy, noisy, self-opinionated and utterly ghastly in every way. The only possibly interesting man was a publisher. Simon, having given up banking, now worked part-time for an Oxford publishers and this was his boss. He was cheerfully erudite and extremely old. However he was more interested in Felicity for her skill as a book illustrator than for her body, mercifully. Still, there was possibly a job in it and that was what Felicity needed at the moment, money being tight, so she made herself pleasant. However, on this last night Gilla had given in to the cries for mercy and the three of them were alone and it was fun. They drank too much and reminisced about old times, and over crème brulées, torched to death by Gilla, who was now thoroughly over-excited, the matter turned to the question of money.

'I'm so glad,' said Simon, 'that I am no longer in banking, I think these are very worrying times.'

'Are they?' Felicity asked. 'I thought the Northern Rock thing was just a glitch. Most people seem to be able to afford whatever they want when they want it, technology becoming cheaper and cheaper and everything easier to achieve. When I left school, for a holiday job before college, I worked in a typing pool for an insurance company. It only lasted for a couple of weeks but it nearly killed me, just typing the same letter over and over. Now that job could be done by one person on a laptop, there were sixty of us. Think how much less companies must be paying on overheads.'

'And think of the fifty-nine people who haven't got a job,' said Simon. 'Banks are over-stretching themselves, are lending money inappropriately and are more concerned with their paper profits than serving the commercial community. It's a high risk strategy that is going to end in disaster.'

Felicity looked at him quizzically. 'Isn't that why you left Hong Kong, because that was your hobby horse then? It hasn't happened though, has it?'

'No,' said Simon, 'but it will, I don't want to go into it, particularly during a jolly evening like this but yes, I left Hong Kong because I wasn't happy with the way the bank was being run. In my view, if the bubble does burst, Carlyon will be one of the first to go, largely because of the way their Hong Kong branch is run. When I joined, the trading floor was the smallest in Carlyon's empire. Now it's the biggest and it's been achieved at the expense of security. The money they have invested is not secure – they could go at any time.'

Gilla stood up and began clearing the plates.

'Are you sure that's not sour grapes talking, darling? They didn't take your advice and yet they're still in business. Sit down Fizzy, I'll do these. You stay and talk to Simon. I'm not too good at all this banking chat, I'll make some coffee.'

'So you really think things are about to go wrong?' Felicity said when Gilla had left the room.

'It will start in America I think, any moment now,' Simon said, then focusing his full attention on Felicity. 'What about you, where are your investments?'

'I don't have any,' said Felicity.

Simon frowned. 'But you must have, Charlie

wouldn't have left you unprovided for, surely?'

'I gave it away,' said Felicity, 'at least most of it.'

'Gave it away, what on earth for?'

Felicity could see the banker in Simon was clearly appalled at the concept of giving away money.

'I gave it to a charity specialising in drug rehabilitation in young people.'

'Why in God's name did you do that, Fizzy? You're a widow for heaven's sake and you could live for years.'

'It was tainted money, Simon,' said Felicity. 'I don't want to talk about it, I haven't even discussed it with Gilla. I sold the house and used some of the proceeds to buy outright my little cottage in St Ives, so I have no mortgage. I bought a new car and what money I could get from selling the contents of the house I've kept because most of the valuable pieces originally belonged to Charlie's mother and had nothing to do with Charlie's activities.'

'I can't believe old Charlie was into dodgy dealing, he was such a straightforward guy,' Simon said.

'He wasn't into dodgy dealing,' said Felicity, 'but as a young man he accepted the equivalent of a bribe. It was all to do with drug trafficking and money laundering based in South Africa. I only found out about it after he was dead but that's why I couldn't touch his money.'

'I think that was extremely foolish,' said Simon.

'If you could have looked at it in no other way, think that if you are able to support yourself in your old age you will never be a burden on the state. It was almost your duty to hang onto the money.'

Felicity shook her head vehemently. 'Sorry Simon, this isn't a conversation I want to prolong any more than you want to talk about your problems in Hong Kong. You asked a question and the answer is this – no I don't have any significant savings. I do earn some money from my art and I work a day a week in the local school and later, of course, I will have my old age pension. Also, although I won't accept money from Mel to look after my own granddaughter, she does cover my expenses.'

'And when you're too old to work any more?'

'Straight off the edge of a Cornish cliff,' said Felicity.

'Or find a man to support you,' said Gilla, coming in with the coffee, 'preferably someone who is not restricted to a policeman's salary.'

'What's that?' Simon asked.

Felicity gave Gilla a murderous look. 'Sorry,' Gilla mouthed.

Felicity left Oxford at 5.30am the following morning. Although it was a Sunday and therefore not a changeover day, being August, she was far from confident that the roads would be clear if she left the journey any later. It was a beautiful morning and as it turned out there was very little traffic. Harvey slept peacefully on the back seat; he would be pleased to be home. Home, it was an interesting word. She had spent most of her life in Oxford, having been to school there, married there, raised her children there. By contrast she had only spent the last six years in Cornwall but it really felt like she was going home. Running away from Cornwall, running away from Keith Penrose, was not the answer. She must buck up and stop feeling sorry for herself. She had so much to be thankful for – two children happily married; two grandsons, a little granddaughter and another one by mid September; a daughter living close by and a wealth of friends in St Ives. Feeling sorry for herself because her relationship with Keith Penrose could not develop further was pathetic. At fifty-three it was surely time to recognise that one couldn't always have what one wanted in life.

Leaving the M5 she turned onto the A30, and forty minutes later she was over the Tamar, into Cornwall and climbing towards Bodmin Moor. Her spirits soared; yes it was good to be home. Her mobile phone jangled making her jump. She glanced down at it. It was Simon – clearly they were ringing to check she arrived safely, no one ever realised how long it took to reach West Cornwall. She had no hands free so she ignored the call, she would ring them when she arrived home. Five minutes later her phone rang again. This second call slightly unnerved Felicity; why ring again, had she forgotten something? She glanced fondly in her rear view mirror, certainly not Harvey. She had packed everything, surely – there was only one small suitcase of belongings. Her walking boots and waxed jacket were in the boot and her handbag was on the passenger seat. She had barely finished her inventory when the phone rang for a third time. 'This is harassment,' she announced to Harvey and seeing a parking area indicated a mile ahead, she drove to it and stopped the car. 'I'll give you a stretch of legs first, they can wait,' she said. She clipped on Harvey's lead and took him out onto the grass verge. While she waited for him to perform his ablutions she heard her mobile phone ring yet again. Maybe Simon's phone was stuck on some sort of redial, that must be it. She would ring him and tell him to stop driving her mad. She offered Harvey a bowl of water and then settled him in the back of the car on his rug with a couple of dog biscuits. With the sound of him crunching contentedly she returned Simon's call. At first she thought she must have the wrong number, the voice that answered was hoarse, broken, trembling and utterly unrecognisable. 'Can I speak to Simon please?' Felicity said, confused.

'Fizzy, Fizzy, is that you?'

'Yes, is that you Simon?'

'Fizzy, she's dead, she's died. Please come back, I can't cope, I don't know what to say to Ellie, I can't … please come.'

* * *

That morning Gilla and Simon had woken early, too. Gilla, a notoriously light sleeper, had been woken by Felicity tiptoeing around the house and on seeing what a beautiful day it was, she had bullied Simon mercilessly until he had finally succumbed and padded off to make them both some coffee.

'Let's go for a walk on Otmoor,' Gilla said, 'we could take a picnic and bottle of wine.'

They were sitting in their conservatory with the Sunday papers spread out. Simon eyed her mischievously over the top of his *Sunday Times*.

'If only we had a dog, it would make it far more fun.'

'Don't mention dogs,' said Gilla, rising immediately to the bait. 'She makes an absolute fool of that little dog; she was the same with that wretched cat.'

'Orlando, as you very well know, is buried in our garden so I think you should show more respect,' said Simon, firmly.

'I just can't understand the fuss she makes over animals, I suppose it's because there isn't a proper man in her life.'

'What was that about a policeman?' Simon asked.

'Mind your own business,' said Gilla, swatting him over the head with a paper as she stood up. 'Now, I don't want you idling around here all morning. I'll go and make some sandwiches and then we can go for a good hike.'

'Do I have to?' Simon asked, plaintively grinning at her.

'Yes, you do,' said Gilla, firmly.

'You're a cruel and heartless woman.'

'I'm not,' said Gilla, 'and I'll tell you why … because you're going to get a reward for all that marching across Otmoor.'

'And what would that be?' Simon asked.

'A siesta,' Gilla grinned at him wickedly. 'Do we have a deal?'

'We certainly do,' Simon said. He hurried through his dressing and shaving routine. If he was quick there would still be time to scan through the financial press – he could feel the trouble brewing, taste it almost. He loved his current life, helping his wife with her business, acting as financial director for a small publishing house, but he was a banker by blood. When he came downstairs he could hear Gilla still bustling around in the kitchen. He went back to the conservatory and settled down with the paper. Minutes passed as he absorbed the news. Then there was the sound of a loud crash. Simon waited for the usual rush of oaths which would inevitably follow, but there were none – just an odd silence.

He put down his paper. 'Gilla, darling.' Nothing. He leapt to his feet and ran to the kitchen. His wife was sprawled on the floor, she was lying on her front with her head turned to one side, her eyes wide open. 'Gilla. Gilla, darling. What's happened, are you alright?' He knelt down and ridiculously picked up one of her hands and began rubbing it between his. 'Gilla, Gilla, speak to me, what's happened?' Her hand felt oddly lifeless, as if all the energy had gone from her. Recovery position, mouth to mouth, they were words he knew but he didn't know what to do, didn't know how to do it. An ambulance – he dashed to the phone and dialled 999. An ambulance was on its way; being in North Oxford they were just minutes from the John Radcliffe Hospital.

'Best not to move her,' the woman said. 'Stay calm, stay by her, if you can make sure her airways are clear, but don't move her, we'll be with you in just a few minutes, you'll hear the siren.'

Simon dropped the phone with trembling hands and rushed back to his wife's side, crouching down on the kitchen floor beside her. He took her hand again and stared into her face. Her sightless eyes stared back at him but she wasn't there, her lovely eyes looked wrong. He loved her eyes, their bright green mesmerised him. He could hear a siren wailing now, coming closer, yet he felt oddly reluctant to go to the door and let in the paramedics, cherishing these last moments alone with his wife for he already knew that they would tell him that there was nothing they could do for her.

3

'Oh, Mum, I'm so, so sorry.'

'It's just awful,' Felicity replied, tearfully, '... the shock, I just can't believe, can't take it in. She looked so well, was so full of life – just like normal.' Felicity was back in Oxford, sitting at the bottom of the stairs in Simon and Gilla's house. Simon was upstairs in their bedroom, sobbing. She could hear him, even down here in the hall; his grief seemed to be totally out of control. She didn't know what to do for him; he was unrecognisable from the confident, self-possessed man she knew. Felicity tried to concentrate on her phone call. She had rung her daughter, Mel, to tell her the news and to explain why she wasn't back in Cornwall. There and then on Bodmin Moor, in response to Simon's call, she had turned around and driven straight back to Oxford.

'You got as far as Bodmin?' Mel was saying. 'Mum, you must be exhausted.'

'Oddly, I'm not,' said Felicity, 'I'm just dreading Ellie's arrival, I can't think of a single word of comfort.

There isn't one, is there, that's the awful truth?'

'When is she coming? Where from?' Mel asked. Although Gilla and Felicity had been best friends, their daughters were not. In fairness there was a big age gap, Mel being eight years older than Ellie, but in truth they had absolutely nothing in common. Mel had been a very active child, and had to exceed at every sport, be captain of every team; Ellie had been severely overweight throughout her childhood and had only recently slimmed down – sport for her was out of the question in any serious way, more a trial than pleasure. They were both clever, but Mel in a flamboyant and fiercely competitive way, while Ellie was quiet and studious.

'She's coming down from Edinburgh. She'd gone back up to University early to study.' Felicity said. 'A friend is bringing her as far as Manchester, the trains are hopeless on Sundays, and she is getting a direct line into Oxford from there. I think I'll have to pick her up, Simon shouldn't be driving anywhere. I just don't know how to comfort her, Mel, I can't believe Gilla is dead, and if I can't, how can she?'

'Ellie's never been the easiest person to communicate with,' Mel said.

'It's not that, I get on with her quite well, normally, but to lose your mother at twenty-one ...' Her voice tailed away.

'Gilla lost her mother young, too, didn't she?' Mel asked.

'Yes, she was even younger than Ellie, she was doing her 'A' levels. Her mother died of cancer.'

'So not a brain haemorrhage like Gilla?'

'No,' said Felicity, 'although we won't know for certain what killed her until there has been a post-mortem. I ...' she hesitated. '... I went to the hospital to see her.'

'Oh Mum, that must have been awful.'

'It was, but strangely comforting because she simply wasn't there. There was a body but no Gilla in it. The doctor I saw, a nice woman, said that if it was a brain haemorrhage, she'll have known nothing. She said that people who survive brain haemorrhages say it's like being hit really hard on the back of the head, wallop, but no pain, there's no time for pain.'

'It's a good way to go then,' said Mel.

'But not at fifty-four,' Felicity replied, quietly.

The following days were harrowing in the extreme. When Felicity picked up Ellie from Oxford station, Ellie asked to be taken first to see her mother before going home to her father. Simon was in such a state when they arrived, they decided immediately to call a doctor who gave him a sedative. Ellie was quiet and controlled but Felicity knew it was not because she wasn't absolutely shattered, it was just her way.

During the days that followed, Felicity was lost in admiration as to how Ellie handled her father, organised the funeral, answered letters and phone calls and employed someone to look after her mother's shop. Felicity helped but it was Ellie who ran the show.

The funeral was held eleven days after Gilla's death. It was a glorious golden day with just a hint of autumn and the church in Woodstock was packed; even Simon and Ellie seemed surprised by the number of mourners. Ellie had tried to make the service as upbeat as possible, a celebration of her mother's life, but she could not overcome the bare facts that here was a woman who loved life, had so much still to offer and had died way too young. Only the family and Felicity, with Jamie, her son, and Mel went on to the dismal business of the crematorium. They had tried to persuade Simon to have people back to the house afterwards, saying a party was what Gilla would have liked, but he couldn't bear it. As soon as they were home, he took himself up to his bedroom. Jamie delivered his sister to Reading station for the long train journey back to Cornwall and Ellie and Felicity were left sitting opposite one another at the kitchen table.

'You know what your mother would do in these circumstances,' said Felicity.

'Open a bottle of wine?' Ellie suggested with a small smile.

'I don't think so, I think champagne would be what she would insist upon and it so happens I have one chilling in the fridge. Shall we open it?'

Ellie nodded, the smile broadened. 'You're right, of course,' she said. 'What a good godmother you are.'

'Hardly that,' said Felicity, fussing around with glasses and popping the cork, 'but I will try, Ellie, to be there for you in any way I can. I am not your mother and never can be but I will try to do anything and everything she would have done for you in the years ahead.'

'Thank you, Fizzy. I'll be alright,' said Ellie, accepting the glass of champagne. 'It's Dad I'm worried about.'

They raised their glasses. 'Gilla, Mum,' they said. They clinked glasses and drank, avoiding each other's eyes, aware that they would see the tears.

'I need to get back up to Edinburgh by the end of the week,' said Ellie, suddenly. 'It sounds really selfish but I think it's the best thing for me. With my final year coming up I really have to get my head down and if I work hard they say I should get a First.' Ellie was reading History at Edinburgh.

'I think it is absolutely the right thing for you, too,' said Felicity. 'Getting back among your friends and your work, you can't pretend this hasn't happened, nor should you, but at least it will show you that life goes on. I know people always say this but it's what your mother would have wanted.'

'I know,' said Ellie, 'but what about Dad? I just don't know what to do for him. I love him, of course,

33

but we've been apart for most of my life and I don't really know how to cope with his grief. I can't help him and he can't help me either. Mum was the glue which held us together. Now we feel miles apart and at the moment I think it is just adding to our unhappiness.'

'I agree,' said Felicity, 'you both need to get over the initial shock and then hopefully by Christmas you will find a way to talk about your feelings.' The thought of Christmas without Gilla was so appalling that Felicity hurried on, '... so, I thought I might try and persuade him to come down to Cornwall with me. What do you think?'

'I think that's a brilliant idea,' said Ellie, 'if you don't mind. You could introduce him to Annie, she might sort him out. Look what she did for me.'

Annie Trethewey had first been Felicity's landlady when she had moved to St Ives and latterly her friend, a no-nonsense little character full of good common sense and not afraid to speak her mind. Felicity smiled to herself; somehow she couldn't see Annie and Simon having too much in common.

Ellie chuckled. 'I know exactly what you're thinking – they're not exactly obvious soulmates, are they?'

Felicity smiled fondly at her goddaughter. 'You know me too well, Ellie,' she said.

The expression on Ellie's face changed from amusement to deep sadness. 'I don't think I've really addressed it yet. Mum was so, well so alive, wasn't she, as far as I'm concerned if I hadn't just gone through the funeral and seen her at the hospital, I'd still be thinking that she was going to walk through the door any moment swinging a bottle of wine and suggesting we all have a party.'

Tears came into Felicity's eyes. She knew she mustn't cry and especially not in front of Ellie. 'That's the perfect way to remember her,' she said, quietly.

'Do you think I'm awful wanting to go back up to university, only I think I've just got to, it's the only way I'm going to survive this?'

'As I said, I think you're doing absolutely the right thing,' said Felicity. 'I think when you're back up there, at times you're going to feel dreadful. Perhaps when you're with friends, out having a good time, or by contrast when you are alone studying, suddenly the whole thing will hit you like a bolt from the blue. However, that's what you have a godmother for – ring me night or day, I can come up and see you or you can come down to Cornwall, or we can meet here – we can talk or e-mail, just promise me you'll keep telling me how you're feeling. Don't bottle it up.'

Ellie nodded. 'I couldn't have got through the last couple of weeks without you.' She suddenly looked very young and very vulnerable.

Felicity stood up, walked around the kitchen table and, crouching down, gave Ellie a small awkward hug. 'I haven't faced up to things either.

Your mother was more than just my best friend, she was like my sister. With neither of us having any siblings of our own, I told her everything. I can't imagine life without her because I've never really known what that would be like.' Her voice sounded bleak, even to herself. She could feel hot tears on her cheeks. She stood up and abruptly turning towards the sink, reached for a piece of kitchen roll and dabbed at her eyes. 'Sorry Ellie,' she said, 'I'm not helping you at all, am I?'

'You've been marvellous.' Ellie came and stood beside her and put an arm around Felicity's shoulders. 'You've been an absolute rock to me and Dad in the last few days, but everyone has been so concerned about Dad losing his wife and me losing my Mum, no one has given a thought to you losing your best friend.'

'I'm fine,' Felicity blew her nose. 'Anyway, let's make a plan. When did you say you wanted to go back up to Edinburgh?'

'At the weekend, I thought,' said Ellie. 'That gives us three days to get Dad geared up to the idea of Cornwall,' she hesitated. 'Fizzy, I can't do anything about Mum's things, I couldn't bear it. Dad won't want me to, will he?'

'No, of course not,' said Felicity. 'I would imagine he'll want everything left as it is for a while and when he's ready to do anything about it, I'll help him if that's what he wants.'

They put their plans to Simon at breakfast the next morning. He had changed out of all recognition over the last two weeks. As well as losing at least a stone in weight, the self-assured, slightly pompous manner of the ex-banker had gone and he had become, quite literally, a shadow of his former self.

Felicity had expected opposition to the idea of a visit to Cornwall but, in fact, he accepted immediately. 'I'm not going to be much fun as a house guest,' he said, 'and I won't stay long, I promise, but it would be good to get away. I simply can't stay here without Gilla.'

'That's what we thought,' Felicity said, smiling at Ellie and seeing the relief on her face. 'Ellie is going to go back up to Edinburgh at the weekend and I thought if we travelled down on Sunday morning we would miss most of the traffic.'

Simon nodded. 'That'll be fine. What day is it today, what day of the week I mean, I'm losing track?'

'It's Thursday,' said Felicity.

'Damn,' said Simon. 'I'm supposed to be having lunch with my old boss today; I'll cancel it, of course.'

'Don't Dad,' said Ellie, 'it might do you good.'

'I don't think lunch with Hugh Randall will do me much good, can't stand the fellow, never have liked him.'

'Why did you agree to meet him then?' Felicity asked.

'He was at the funeral. It was decent of him to

come, I accept that. After the service, he suggested that we had lunch today and I was so, well, distraught I'd have agreed to anything.'

'Where did he suggest you met?' Felicity asked.

'Well actually, Les Quat' Saisons.'

'Dad, you cannot turn down lunch at the Quat' Saisons,' Ellie said, smiling. 'I'll drive you there.'

'You don't need to,' Simon replied with the ghost of a smile, 'he said he'd send a car for me at midday.'

'Goodness me, he's really putting out the red carpet for you, isn't he? said Felicity. 'Nice of him I suppose, trying to cheer you up, he can't be all bad, Simon.'

Simon shook his head. 'No, Hugh Randall never does anything for nothing. There will be a hidden agenda and I have a feeling I know exactly what it is.'

Simon being occupied with his lunch date and Ellie planning to spend the day with a school friend meant that for the first time since Gilla's death Felicity had some time on her hands. Something had been nagging at the back of her mind since the funeral. Among the many mutual friends who had attended had been Josh Buchanan, with whom she had been barely able to exchange a word such had been her preoccupation with supporting Simon and Ellie. Josh had been her husband's partner in their law practice. Some years younger than Charlie Paradise, Josh had been the junior partner. Now he ran the practice himself with a junior partner called Simms. During their Oxford years Gilla and Josh had been very regular visitors to the Paradises' home in Norham Gardens. Gilla as a single parent, following her disastrous break-up with Simon, had needed a great deal of support. Josh, after a brief failed marriage, had been very much the man about town. Good-looking, charming, there was always a girl on his arm but he seemed unable to make another serious commitment and had remained single. Like Gilla, he appeared to use Norham Gardens as an emotional prop. He never bought his girls to the house and seemed to relish family life, happily mucking in with the children and clearly full of admiration for Charlie.

The mutual support which should have followed Charlie Paradise's death had not happened because Felicity had discovered that Josh had been complicit in keeping from her the tangled web in which Charlie had involved himself and which ultimately had led to his death. Felicity felt she could no longer trust him and without trust there could be no true friendship. Now, however, the dynamics had changed again with Gilla's death. There had been so many happy evenings spent by the four of them in Norham Gardens. They had known each other so well, grown up together, shared birthdays, Christmases, small triumphs, small disappointments. They had been easy with one another; there had been so much fun and laughter. Now there was only her and Josh left and she had an overriding desire to talk to him, despite all her misgivings about him as a person.

She telephoned the familiar number and was put straight through. 'Josh, it's Fizzy.'

He let out a great sigh of relief. 'Thank God,' he said, 'I was hoping you would ring, I didn't like to add to your obvious burdens but I so need to talk to you.'

Felicity felt tears prick her eyes. 'I so need to talk to you too.'

'I imagine you're worn out with caring, aren't you?' Josh asked.

'Something like that,' Felicity managed, between her tears. 'Are you free for lunch, Josh?

'Of course I am,' said Josh. 'Where shall we go, Browns?'

'I don't do Browns,' said Felicity. There was puzzled silence for a minute. 'Charlie was killed almost outside the door, remember.'

'Of course,' said Josh, 'sorry. Look I'll pick you up and let's get out of town. Why don't we go to the Trout at Godstow? It's a nice day, we could sit by the river.'

'That would be good,' said Felicity.

At the sound of Josh's car, Felicity slipped like a fugitive from the house and was into the passenger seat before Josh even had time to get out of the car. She had left no one in the house, apart from Harvey. Simon had already been picked up for his lunch date and Ellie had long gone to visit her friend. It was the first time she had been alone in the house and she had found Gilla's lingering presence both unsettling and sad.

With unusual sensitivity Josh did not say a word. He bent over, pecked her cheek, grasped her hand and then letting go, slid the car into gear and drove straight out of the driveway. It took just a few minutes to drive down the Woodstock Road, turn left along Port Meadow and so to Godstow. Josh pulled into the pub car park, passed gnarled old trees and parked in a discreet corner. He turned off the engine, turned to Felicity and held out his arms. She came to him immediately and began to cry, big uncontrollable sobs that racked her body. He simply held her and said nothing, recognizing there were no words of comfort, that there was nothing good to say about Gilla's death. At last, Felicity's sobs quietened and she started to gain control. Josh produced a handkerchief and she began mopping her face, gradually pulling herself away from his embrace.

'I'm so sorry,' she said, 'I've made a nasty mess of your suit.'

'It couldn't matter less,' said Josh. 'Is that the first time you've been able to cry properly about Gilla?'

Felicity nodded. 'I've had to hold myself together for Simon and Ellie, I'd have been useless to them if I'd let go. I'm sorry you've had to be the recipient of all this.'

'I'm the right person,' said Josh and Felicity realised that despite everything, it was true.

She fumbled about in her bag and produced a mirror. 'Oh God,' she said, 'what a sight.'

'Not at all,' said Josh, gallantly.

'Liar!' Felicity repaired her face as best she could then she turned to Josh. 'I don't think I can cope with people yet, could we just have a walk down the towpath before going to lunch?'

'I was going to suggest the same thing myself,' said Josh. He took her hand and they walked over the little humpback bridge and onto the towpath beside the river.

'And then there were two,' Felicity said, quietly.

Josh squeezed her hand. 'That's what I've been thinking. Who would have imagined six years ago, the four of us sitting around the table at Norham Gardens sharing a bottle of wine, that such a thing could happen?'

'It's odd, isn't it,' said Felicity, 'of the four of us, they were the two who were larger than life, more flamboyant than us.'

'Noisier certainly,' said Josh.

Felicity let out a laugh. 'Charlie and Gilla's arguments, now they were dramatic affairs!'

'She used to think up topics just to irritate him, didn't she?' said Josh.

'Absolutely, goading Charlie was one of Gilla's favourite pastimes and he loved it, of course – they never tired of baiting one another.'

'How many years were you at Norham Gardens?'

'We were married for twenty-three years,' said Felicity, 'so the four of us were certainly getting together on a regular basis for well over twenty years.'

'That's a big chunk of life,' said Josh, pausing to look at a moorhen swimming fussily about at the water's edge.

'The biggest really,' said Felicity, 'I feel that those middle years of life are the most vivid – childhood and adolescence is the build-up to it and then when you get to the age I am now, you're in decline. It's the middle bit that counts most.'

'Don't say that Fizzy, you have years ahead of you yet.'

'Very possibly,' said Felicity, 'although one feels somewhat vulnerable, like being in the front line. With Gilla's death nothing seems certain anymore.'

'That's true,' said Josh, taking her hand again and continuing to walk. 'How's old Simon doing?'

'Not well,' said Felicity, 'he's out to lunch today with his former boss. I'm hoping that might cheer him up a bit, give him something else to think about but he's completely fallen apart, poor chap.'

'It's not helped by the fact that he's, well how do I put it, he's so awfully dull with no resources to fall back on,' Josh ventured.

'Oh Josh, that's not fair, he's not dull, he's just not as vibrant as Gilla.'

'Few people are,' Josh said, 'though I have to say I never understood what she saw in him, those two were like chalk and cheese. I'd have thought poor old Simon would have bored her rigid in five minutes.'

'Opposites attract,' Felicity suggested.

'But not that opposite,' Josh said.

'You're not being very kind given all the circumstances,' Felicity suggested.

'No, you're right, but I can't imagine you've been able to have any cosy chats with him about how he's feeling and that sort of thing, have you?'

'No,' Felicity admitted, 'I haven't and what worries me is how hard it is for Ellie to get through to him as well.'

'They were apart for so many years, weren't they? They haven't got much of a relationship to fall back on.'

'Ellie said that Gilla was the glue that held them together.'

'Good way of putting it,' said Josh, 'bright girl, Ellie.'

'Yes, she is,' said Felicity, 'and a very nice one too, but she's not getting much emotional support from her father now nor, I have to say, can I imagine things changing very much in the future. He'll always look after her in a practical sense, make sure she has enough money, somewhere to live and all that sort of thing but there is no obvious emotional bond between them. I expect Gilla was probably the only person who really got through to Simon, I certainly can't.'

By mutual consent they turned around and started walking back along the towpath towards the pub.

'Well, we're Ellie's godparents, aren't we?' said Josh, 'we're going to have to do our best to fill the gap left by Gilla.'

'Yes,' said Felicity. 'Josh, it is good to know you think like that, I was feeling rather isolated.'

'You're not alone,' Josh said reassuringly, 'I promise. Between us we'll do whatever we can for Ellie.'

They stepped through the ancient doorway into the pub garden.

'Oh, it's years since I've been here,' said Felicity, 'I'd forgotten how lovely it is.'

The Trout at Godstow was on the site of what had once been a monastery. It is said that somewhere towards the end of the twelfth century, twelve learned men got together at the monastery and dreamt up the idea of Oxford University. There was certainly a sense of history about the place and the peacocks strutting around the garden enhanced the atmosphere. It suited their mood. Josh ordered drinks and a salad and they sat down by the river watching the trout jumping about in the tumbling water while the swans looked on disdainfully from the calmer shallows.

'Are you still angry with me?' Josh asked.

Felicity studied him in silence for a moment. 'I

did feel very let down, Josh, I can't pretend I didn't, but set against the backdrop of Gilla's death, it all seems less important. You are right about Ellie, we do have a joint responsibility. How about us drawing a double line under everything that's gone before and starting again, for Ellie's sake.'

'I'll drink to that,' said Josh and they raised glasses silently to one another.

Josh dropped Felicity back to Simon and Gilla's home shortly before three. There was no sign of either Simon or Ellie and a quick inspection of the fridge showed it to be lamentably empty. Loading a sulking Harvey into the car Felicity set off for Summertown and some serious food shopping. An hour later, she staggered back into the kitchen piled high with carrier bags loaded with delicious bits and pieces with which she hoped to tempt Simon back to eating and to life over the next few days.

At first she thought she was alone in the house and then she saw him through the kitchen window, sitting under a tree in the garden, apparently deep in thought. She made two mugs of tea and carried them out, handing Simon his and sitting on the grass at his feet.

'How was your lunch?' she asked.

'Marvellous, I suppose, only rather wasted on me. My taste buds seem to have died with Gilla and in any event we weren't having the kind of conversation that was conducive to concentrating on the quality of the food.'

Felicity glanced up at him and frowned. 'Why on earth did he ask you out to lunch then, if it wasn't to cheer you up?'

'Oh, it doesn't matter,' Simon said, dismissively. There was a long silence. Felicity was used to Simon's long silences at the best of times and began thinking what she was going to cook for supper and whether Ellie would be back in time.

It came as a surprise when Simon suddenly spoke.

'Actually Fizzy, it would be helpful if I could just talk this through with you if you wouldn't mind?'

'Of course not,' Felicity said, thinking that if nothing else, a conversation that didn't revolve around Gilla had to be a good thing for him, for both of them.

'It's a banking story,' said Simon, 'so you'll probably find it dull, but I'll try to keep it as brief as possible. You'll remember I went to Hong Kong?'

Felicity nodded, not daring to speak – knowing both of them were acutely aware of why he had gone abroad so abruptly.

'It was in early 1990,' Simon said, 'and circumstances apart, it was an exciting job opportunity for me. Up until then, I had always worked for the major clearing banks, carving a good career, steadily climbing the ladder but nothing exciting. Then...' he hesitated, 'then Gilla and I had our problems and I started looking around for something which would totally absorb me. I applied for a job with the Carlyon Bank as Financial Controller in the Far East. I thought it would be good to get away.' A look of pain swept over his face.

It is so unfair, Felicity thought – having been reconciled after so many years apart, they had so few years together, he and Gilla.

'Anyway, I got the job,' said Simon, pulling himself together visibly. 'I was responsible for the whole of the Far East but was based in Hong Kong and although I missed Gilla and Ellie, I found it totally absorbing, loved it actually. Carlyon was at a very exciting stage. It had just been bought out by a group of merchant bankers and under their expertise it was flourishing and developing internationally, particularly in Hong Kong where there was huge growth.'

'Why do I have a feeling that this story is not going to have a happy ending?' Felicity said.

'I'm coming to that,' said Simon. 'It took me several years to really get my feet under the table and understand how the business worked. Hugh Randall, the man I met today was, and still is, Chairman of the Board based in the UK and my ultimate boss. However, in the Far East I was working under a chap called Tony Wong, an impressive guy, very dynamic, younger than me, with fantastic contacts just about everywhere. The years went by and we continued to prosper. However, as Financial Controller, I began to worry about the type of investments the bank was making out of Hong Kong.'

'What were they, dodgy?' Felicity asked.

'Dodgy in the sense that it seemed to me there were some gaping holes in the asset value – in other words the investments appeared impressive on paper but in fact were pretty worthless. It concerned me how fast the Hong Kong arm was growing. Tony Wong and his number one investment broker – a chap called Alex Button – were drawing enormous bonuses which was fair enough based on their performance but I became increasingly unhappy about it, when linked to the health of the bank.' Simon paused and sipped his tea. 'I did some digging around and sure enough managed to piece together a report which demonstrated there was a deep black hole where there should have been assets to support the Bank's investments.'

'Goodness, what did you do?' Felicity asked.

'I flew to London and had a meeting with Hugh Randall. I gave him my report, told him to think about it and offered to stay in a hotel in London overnight while he did so. He said I'd need to stay in town a couple of nights because he had wall-to-wall meetings. On the spur of the moment I rang Gilla and told her I was in England. She suggested I came down to Oxford and that we had some supper.' He smiled at Felicity sadly. 'I never used that hotel room,' he said.

Felicity put out a hand and touched one of his, squeezing it.

'By the time I met Hugh Randall again two days later, I was feeling great. Suddenly my life was in perspective. Yes of course I cared about my job but it was just that, a job. I had got Gilla back, I felt full of confidence. I went into the meeting expecting him to thank me for my work and say he would sort out Wong and Button. I even wondered if I might be offered the Chairmanship of Hong Kong, I could have handled it, though I was not sure I wanted it now, because of Gilla.'

'But?' Felicity asked.

'But instead,' said Simon, 'he sacked me.'

'Oh my God,' said Felicity, 'could he do that?'

'Probably not,' said Simon.

'What were his reasons?'

'He wanted my findings hushed up so essentially he bought me off. I'm not very proud of this, Fizzy, I think I should have stuck to the moral high ground but at the time I was just so damn happy, I didn't ...' his voice tailed off.

'So what,' said Felicity, 'he offered you a lot of money to resign?'

'A redundancy package, full pension rights, the works, in return for my silence – no going to the press, no going to anyone.'

'I don't think there is anything to feel guilty about over that,' said Felicity. 'You found out there were problems in Hong Kong and you alerted the Chairman of the Bank. If he chose to ignore you and pay you off to keep quiet, that's his decision – you'd done your job.'

'If Gilla and I hadn't just got back together again I think I might have brazened it out, stuck to my guns, demanded an enquiry, reported my findings to the FSA and gone to the press with whatever was necessary to expose those guys in Hong Kong. However, suddenly I could only see what a marvellous opportunity being sacked presented. I could stay in the UK, see Gilla and Ellie all the time. I didn't even have to find a job, the pay-off was that good. Gilla told me you were very angry with her for sleeping with that guy, but in her defence, I was working such long hours I was never there for her. She had a small baby, she was someone who needed people around her and I failed her. In truth, I think I should have been thinking of my duty to the bank shareholders but I could only see that Hugh Randall was giving me the chance to try and put things right with my wife and daughter.'

'And you have,' Felicity said. 'It's a tragedy you had so little time together but you made her so wonderfully happy.'

Simon looked in Felicity's eyes. 'Yes, I think I did. We have been very happy over the last few years,

51

with me working part-time and helping her with the shop. The work-fun balance has been just about right, particularly for someone like Gilla.'

There was a painful silence. 'And so,' Felicity said at last, 'you took the money and met your part of the deal which meant saying nothing to anyone.'

'And nor have I,' said Simon, 'to no one, ever, until today, to you.'

'And so why are you telling me all this now?' Felicity asked.

'At lunch today Hugh Randall didn't beat about the bush. Carlyon are in trouble and they are in trouble because of the toxic assets they have acquired mostly in Hong Kong. They have invested billions of pounds without sufficient assets to support them. They have been trying to find a major bank to buy them out but it appears that most of the banks are in trouble at the moment so they are going for a Government bail-out. Hugh wanted to make sure that I was not going to cause trouble. If the Chancellor learnt that the Board had been advised several years ago that things weren't as they should be, it might affect his decision.'

'So are you going to spill the beans?' Felicity asked.

'I don't think so, though I'm not happy about the idea of taxpayers supporting a bank which clearly has been trading fraudulently for some years by not disclosing its true position.' He hesitated. 'Hugh asked me if I still had a copy of the report which I gave him.'

'What did you say?' Felicity said.

'I told him I haven't.'

'And have you?' Felicity asked.

Simon looked at her, solemnly. 'Yes, of course I have.'

4

Travelling south-west again, this time with Simon beside her, Felicity's thoughts were full of Gilla. It was two weeks to the day since she had made the journey before, so blissfully unaware at the time that Gilla was living her final moments of life. During the journey Simon was either silent or asleep and Felicity was relieved – neither of them had the emotional stamina for small talk. By Taunton, she was aware of how tired she was feeling so she stopped and gave Harvey a walk while Simon bought them coffee but this little break was the only time they spoke during the whole journey. By the time they dropped down into St Ives, the bay laid out before them, Felicity was exhausted and it was still only 10.30. It was however, very good to be home.

Because the September festival was in full swing, the town was crammed with visitors and Felicity had plenty to do. She made up the bed in the spare room for Simon, went shopping and bought enough food for a couple of days, walked an overjoyed Harvey around the Island and then she settled Simon on the balcony with a beer and a newspaper while she cooked a late lunch. They had their lunch, a seafood risotto with salad, sitting on the balcony in the sunshine overlooking the town and the harbour.

'This is absolutely magic,' said Simon. He had never visited Felicity in St Ives before; Gilla had always come alone, or with Ellie.

'It is special,' Felicity said, 'and I can't ever imagine taking it for granted.'

'I had absolutely no idea what to expect. No wonder you were happy to leave Oxford. It's so different here, almost like another country.'

'If you ask any Cornishman, he'll tell you it is another country,' Felicity smiled, 'and yes, it is good to be home.'

'I can see this is home for you now,' said Simon as he gazed around him, 'and why would it not be, it's absolutely beautiful.'

After lunch, by mutual consent, they retired to their respective rooms for a siesta in deference to their early start. When Felicity woke it was early evening. She knocked tentatively on Simon's door but the room was empty, he had clearly gone for a walk.

She took the opportunity of being alone to ring Mel. 'How are you feeling, darling?' she asked.

'Just about ready to pop. God, this pregnancy

thing is one awful conspiracy, isn't it?'

'What do you mean?' Felicity asked.

Mel laughed. 'Well, you forget don't you, you're somehow anaesthetised. You completely blank out how awful it is to be pregnant and how painful giving birth is until it's too late. Clearly we've been hard wired to do so in order that we go on producing the species.'

Felicity said. 'I do remember that with you, actually, waddling down to the delivery suite thinking why am I going through this again, what on earth possessed me, but think of the end product. In my case it was definitely worth it – look at you!'

'No one would want to look at me at the moment,' said Mel. 'I am truly huge this time, Mum. I can't get comfortable whatever I do. If I stand up everything aches, if I sit down I'm uncomfortable because I squash my tummy and when I lie down everything flops from one side to the other, it's awful.'

'How's my little Minty?' Felicity asked, referring to her granddaughter.

'Missing Granny, I've told her you were back in Cornwall. Would you and Simon like to come over to lunch tomorrow?'

'I think I'll give him a day to settle in,' said Felicity, 'he's all over the place at the moment. I'll certainly ask him if he'd like to come on Tuesday, if that's all right with you, but he might not be up to it.'

'Poor chap,' said Mel, 'I still can't believe it –

Gilla, of all people.'

'Don't,' said Felicity, 'that's what we're all feeling, I think. It just feels so impossible that someone so full of life one minute can be dead the next. It certainly makes one face one's own mortality. I know you're having a beastly time, darling, but I am so grateful to Minty's little brother or sister. He or she is all about the future, new life – very comforting just at this moment.'

'Good,' said Mel, 'I'm very glad you and Martin are so happy about it. As for me right now, I'd be very happy if Minty was an only child.'

'Two weeks from now, it'll be a very different story.'

'No it won't,' said Mel, 'admittedly, I'll no longer resemble Truro Cathedral but think of all the leaking boobs and lack of sleep – it's a nightmare.'

'I'll be there,' said Felicity, 'to help in any way I can.'

'Thanks Mum. Do you think Simon will still be with you? I rather selfishly hope he won't.'

'I've no idea,' said Felicity. 'One day at a time, I think. I'll see you on Tuesday, if you're sure. Would you like me to bring food?'

'No, no, it's alright, I've got nothing else to do. Just bring yourself and Simon if you can.'

'I'll let you know when I've spoken to him,' said Felicity. She had barely replaced the receiver, when the phone rang again. Frowning, she picked it up. She had wanted a little quiet time in her home before Simon returned.

'Is that Mrs Paradise?'

'Yes,' said Felicity.

'It's June here,' Felicity tried to get her brain in gear. 'Mrs Carter's cleaner,' the voice added helpfully in its soft Oxfordshire burr.

Of course, lovely June who had been so helpful over the last couple of weeks; somehow Oxford seemed so far away now. 'It's so kind of you to ring, June,' Felicity said. 'Simon is out at the moment, having a walk I think. Were you ringing to see if he arrived in one piece?'

'Well no, not really, though I'm glad you had a safe journey.' June's voice was hesitant.

'What can I do for you?' Felicity asked.

'There's been a burglary, at the house.'

'Oh God, no, that's all Simon needs.'

'It's not too serious, Mrs Paradise. Maybe I disturbed them because they only went into one room, Mr Carter's study. I've checked the rest of the house and it's completely untouched and there's nothing missing.'

'When was this?' Felicity asked. 'We only left this morning.'

'It must have been some time this afternoon, after you left and before I arrived. I'd said to Mr Carter I'd pop in this evening.'

'And you say nothing much was taken?' Felicity

repeated.

'No, well I don't think so. All the desk drawers have been opened and papers are scattered around, he's not going to be happy about that. It's a mess but there's no obvious damage.'

'How did they get in?' Felicity asked.

'They must have come over the back wall and through the back door, broke a panel of glass – Mrs Carter has never been one for alarms, more often than not she forgot to lock the house up, she'd never have managed an alarm, bless her.' There was a break in June's voice.

'Have you called the police?' Felicity asked.

'I've reported it although they're not much interested, I don't think. They're certainly not coming round tonight, they've told me just to leave everything as it is and they'll be over in the morning. I've arranged to meet them at the house at ten o'clock.'

'That's very kind of you,' said Felicity. 'Do you think Simon should come back?'

'No, I absolutely don't,' June said firmly. 'If the whole house had been done over that would have been another thing but it's just the one room and, as I said, there's no damage and once the police have been, I can clear it up. I won't be able to put everything back where he'd want it but I can certainly make this look presentable for his return. He needs that holiday with you. You mustn't let him come back.'

'I agree,' said Felicity. 'OK, so will you call us in the morning when the police have been?'

'Yes, of course, I'm sorry to be the bearer of bad news, on top of everything else.'

'Thanks for your help,' said Felicity and replaced the phone. She was still sitting at the table ten minutes later when Simon came wandering up the stairs.

'I feel better for a walk,' he began, then he saw her face. 'What is it Fizzy, what's happened, is it Ellie?'

'No, no, it's just there's been a break-in at your house.'

'What?' He sank into the chair opposite her. 'Oh God, I don't believe it. What have they taken, they haven't touched Gilla's things?'

'No, so far as June can tell nothing much has been taken at all. They've made a mess of your study but they've left the rest of the house untouched. Even in your study June says nothing's damaged, just some papers thrown around.'

'When did she ring?'

'Just now.' Seeing his stricken face she got up, walked round and put her hand on his shoulder. 'Come on, I know this is awful on top of Gilla, but it could have been so much worse. I'll fix you a drink – whisky?' Simon nodded. She poured him a hefty tumbler and going to the fridge helped herself to a glass of white wine.

'Just the study?' Simon repeated.

'Absolutely.'

'Does June know when it happened?'

Felicity shook her head. 'No, she wondered if she might have disturbed them because they had only been in the one room but she really has no idea.' Felicity set down her wine glass. 'I'll start some supper.'

'No, no don't,' said Simon, 'I've booked supper at Porthmeor Beach Café, tapas and things, is that alright?'

'That's very kind of you,' said Felicity.

'Kind?' said Simon. 'When I think what you've done for me over the last three weeks, I'm certainly not going to have you slaving over a hot stove day after day while I'm staying here. The least I can do is to take you out for a few meals. The table is booked in half an hour, is that alright?'

A couple of hours later they were sitting over coffee and the remains of their wine looking out over Porthmeor Beach.

'The evenings are drawing in already; I can't believe the summer is nearly over.'

'That's because you spent so much of it in Oxford,' said Simon.

'I suppose so.' They were silent for a moment, watching the surfers, the tide now well in. 'They'll have to stop in a moment,' said Felicity, 'or else they'll all be hurting themselves, it's called a beach break.'

'What's called a beach break?' Simon asked.

'When the tide is this far in and the waves are short like they are now, the sea can throw the surfers hard up onto the beach and they can do themselves all sorts of damage. It's time they were stopping.'

'My goodness, I didn't realise you were a surfer.'

'I'm not,' said Felicity, 'I occasionally venture out on a body board but my knowledge is all secondhand from my son-in-law, Martin. I was half expecting to see him out here tonight, it looks like the surf has been perfect.'

'Another thing I'm never going to achieve in my life,' Simon said, with a smile, then the smile faded. 'We had so many plans, you know, Gilla and I. Things we were going to do, places to go, I'll never have the heart to do them now, there is no point without her.'

Felicity placed her hand on his. 'I've been through this too you know and when people tell you that time heals and all that rubbish, you want to thump them, but the fact is, you do adjust and you do learn to live again and you do just have to give it time.'

'I was thinking about you when I was on my walk this evening, which is why I booked this table. Has it brought it all back to you, Charlie's death I mean, which was just as sudden as Gilla's? You must just feel it's history repeating itself.'

'Mercifully, I don't think I've had time to think

it through,' Felicity admitted. 'I'm missing Gilla every second of every day, but I've so much to do. I have you and Ellie to worry about and that's absorbed most of my conscious thinking and then there's Mel's baby going to pop out at any moment. I have thought about the similarities with Charlie but only in relation to understanding how you must be feeling, that awful sense of being half of a whole.'

Simon squeezed her hand. 'It feels right to be here,' he said, 'but I won't stay for too long and get in the way of your life. I have a feeling that once you get rid of me it will give you the opportunity to do your own grieving. You'll tell me when I'm in the way, won't you? I won't stay more than a week or two, I promise.'

'Stay as long as you like, Simon, and I mean that,' Felicity replied. 'Your home has always been mine and now the reverse applies. Stay as long as you like and come back whenever you feel like it.' There was a comfortable silence between them. 'The break-in,' Felicity said. 'Have you thought about it?'

'Yes,' said Simon.

'And are you thinking it might be linked to your lunch with the awful Hugh?'

'It could be,' said Simon, 'but it seems rather extreme.'

'You must admit though, it is odd that with a houseful of nice things and televisions and the sort of stuff people steal, they should have chosen your study to do over.' She clapped her hand over her mouth. 'What about your computer?'

'It's a laptop,' said Simon, 'and I have it with me.'

'And the copy of that report?'

'I have that with me, too.'

'Do you, why? Did you think this might be going to happen?'

'No,' said Simon, 'I didn't at all but when I was packing last night I suddenly thought it would quite interesting to read it through, just to remind myself as to what I said. I can't remember much of the detail now, so I simply lifted the file and put it in my suitcase. It's still somewhere stored on my laptop, too, I should imagine.'

'So if that's what they came for they didn't have much luck,' Felicity said.

The next few days passed pleasantly enough. An irate June rang the following morning to say that the police spent all of five minutes in Simon's study and said that since nothing obvious had been taken, there was little they could do. June's husband had repaired the back door and that appeared to be the end of it.

On Tuesday they had the arranged lunch with Mel. Minty, now nearly two and a half, was on cracking form. She took an instant liking to Simon and spent most of the time sitting on his knee and demanding that he played with her. Simon seemed to welcome the diversion and Felicity found it oddly touching – the big bear of a man sitting awkwardly on the floor utterly absorbed in Minty's little games.

She was so bossy. 'No Simon, not like that, put it there.'

'Sorry,' Simon said, humbly.

'He's so good with her, isn't he,' Mel whispered as she and Felicity were clearing away the meal.

'It makes me feel very sad actually,' Felicity said.

'Why?' Mel asked.

'Ellie was just two when Simon and Gilla's marriage broke up – already Minty is at an age when Simon had no contact with his daughter.'

'Did Gilla stop him seeing her then?' Mel was clearly shocked.

'No, no,' said Felicity. 'He just took himself off to Hong Kong. He was so hurt I think, and so he made no attempt to see them again. He sent money of course, he was very good like that, but I don't think it was until Ellie reached the teenage years and started asking about him that they began exchanging letters. I don't think father and daughter met for about fifteen years; in fact I know they didn't.'

'How awful,' said Mel, 'and awful for Ellie too. Minty would be devastated without Martin in her life.'

'A very different situation though,' said Felicity, 'Martin is so hands-on. Even before he went away, Simon worked hideously long hours in the City, I expect Ellie saw very little of him in reality.'

'Still, it's hard,' said Mel, 'particularly, as you say, seeing him now with Minty.'

They had barely walked through the door of Felicity's cottage after lunch with Mel when the phone started ringing.

'Hello, Mrs Paradise, it's June here.' God, thought Felicity, why can't the woman leave us alone? Surely it is not too much to expect Simon to be left in peace for a few days.

'Hello, June,' she said, with studied patience. 'What is it, what can I do for you?'

'I think I might have done the wrong thing.'

'Why?'

'Well, we had this reporter around from the *Oxford Mail* today, asking about the burglary. He was very insistent he wanted to talk to Mr Carter so I gave him Mr Carter's mobile number.'

Felicity's heart skipped a beat. 'And did you tell him where Mr Carter was?'

'Well, not exactly,' said June, 'but I did say he was on holiday with you in Cornwall, well in St Ives. Did I do the wrong thing?'

'No, no, that's fine,' said Felicity. 'Just don't tell anyone else where we are, will you? What Mr Carter needs is a complete rest.'

She had just put down the phone as Simon climbed the stairs from his bedroom. 'Who was that?' he asked.

'June.'

'Oh God, please don't tell me we've been burgled again.'

'No, no, it's odd though.'

'Why, what's happened?' Simon asked.

'June says a reporter had been around from the *Oxford Mail* and she gave him your mobile number.'

'Is that so odd?' said Simon.

'Oh, come on,' said Felicity. 'I know you're a very important ex-banker but what self-respecting reporter from the *Oxford Mail* would waste time over one ransacked study? It just wouldn't be worth the paper it's written on, it's barely a crime. Whoever it was who called round to your house, it certainly wasn't a reporter.'

'This policeman friend of yours who Gilla kept talking about, you don't think he's infected you with an over-developed sense of the dramatic?'

Felicity ignored him. 'June also told him where you were, that you were on holiday in St Ives with me.'

'So you think this is something to do with the Bank? Honestly, Fizzy, I think you're getting rather carried away.'

'Well, we'll see, won't we,' said Felicity. 'Either he's a genuine reporter in which case you'll receive a phone call in the next few hours, or else he's after that report and not a reporter at all, in which case, I suppose we should expect a visitor.'

Simon smiled. 'Well, at least we have Harvey to protect us.'

'This might not be a joking matter, Simon,' Felicity said, firmly.

'Look, dear Fizzy, I know you're trying to find ways to take my mind off Gilla but I think you're going a bit far.'

'I do hope you're right,' Felicity replied, sternly.

5

While the weather in August had been decidedly patchy, now September had arrived there was day after day of glorious sunshine. Felicity was so pleased for Simon. He had begun swimming every day and walking the cliff path, usually dragging her and Harvey in tow. Once a day, either for lunch or supper, he insisted on taking her out. For several hours at a time Felicity could put Gilla to the back of her mind, then the thought of her dead friend would come flashing back. She knew Simon was going through the same process. He would come out of the sea laughing and invigorated and then a shadow would cross his face and he was plunged back into the nightmare of it all. He was looking better though – fitter, tanned, in fact better than Felicity had ever seen him. The weight he had lost immediately after Gilla's death had not come back. Watching him dispassionately one night while he was talking idly to a couple at the bar of the Sloop while he was waiting to be served, Felicity could see he was a very good-looking man –

not for her, never for her, he was Gilla's, but he would find someone else, she was sure of it. She hoped so and she knew Gilla would hope so too.

Simon had been staying for just over a week when he announced that they were to have lunch at the Porthminster Beach Café.

'I do feel spoilt,' said Felicity.

'I've checked it out and it's marvellous. We'll have lunch on the terrace and a swim first, what do you say?'

'I'll have to leave Harvey behind, dogs aren't allowed on the beach.'

'It won't do him any harm; we can take him for a walk later. Come on, we deserve a treat.'

They had a marvellous swim. Felicity, lying on her back and gazing across the harbour towards the town, thought there was really nowhere else on earth, at that moment, she would rather be. They towelled themselves dry and realising they were already late for lunch, dashed into the beach loos to change. Felicity studied herself in the cracked mirror. She had managed to acquire a tan in the last few days so there was no need for make-up. She slapped on a touch of lipstick and ran a comb through her damp hair; she only had on cropped jeans and a t-shirt, she wasn't looking very smart – oh well. They met in the restaurant and were shown through to the terrace.

'I've booked a table right by the sea,' said Simon.

'Fantastic,' said Felicity, taking his hand. 'You are kind.' They walked hand in hand out onto the terrace. There was a couple sitting at the table right in front of them. Felicity glanced in their direction and found herself staring into the bright blue eyes of Chief Inspector Keith Penrose. Felicity dropped Simon's hand as though it burnt her. Keith Penrose inclined his head towards Felicity but made no attempt to greet her or to introduce himself to Simon or her to his companion who must, Felicity realised, be his wife. For a moment she stood like a rabbit caught in the headlights, Simon having gone ahead of her.

'Come on Fizz, what are you doing?' She dragged her eyes away from Keith and walked over to her table. She tried to sit with her back to the Penroses' table but Simon insisted on her facing towards them so that she had a good view of the town. Keith she could see in profile; his wife Barbara seemed to be looking straight at her and in a none-too-friendly way. As the waitress handed her a menu, Felicity saw her hand was trembling as she took it. She stole another glance towards their table. She was right, Barbara Penrose was staring straight at her and the look was fairly hostile – no, very hostile – it was unnerving. Barbara surprised her. She was nice-looking in a severe, sharp-featured way but considerably overweight and she seemed so wrong for Keith. She was formally dressed in a dress and jacket which was

71

totally out of place on Porthminster Beach, her grey hair was scraped back into a neat chignon but she looked more like somebody from the 1950s than today. That should please me, Felicity thought, if she's my rival. Yet oddly it didn't. Keith needs to be with someone cosier, kinder, someone I could never hurt. She stared with unseeing eyes at the menu.

'So what are you going to have?' Simon asked.

'Oh, I don't know,' said Felicity, 'you choose.'

'That's not like you Fizzy, you always have an opinion on everything.' Simon smiled at her. 'What's up?'

'Nothing,' said Felicity, 'I'm fine, but you promised me pampering today and part of the pampering is I don't want to have to make any decisions at all.'

Their order was taken. Keith and Barbara were already at the pudding stage, Felicity was relieved to see – at least Keith was toying with a coffee while Barbara was working her way through a large ice-cream concoction. Simon ordered wine and their starters arrived. Felicity ate mechanically, her mind was reeling. I must look such a fright, she thought. She was covered in sand, sticky with salt and she found that being so close to Keith and not even being able to speak to him was unbearable. I'll go to the loo, she thought. Making her excuses to Simon, she shot past Keith's table like a bullet out of a gun and ran down the stairs into the loo. Once inside she leant against the door and let out a big sigh. I'm behaving like a soppy teenager, this is ridiculous. She stared at her reflection in the mirror, it wasn't too bad. She'd take a few deep breaths and then go back. With a bit of luck Keith and Barbara would be leaving. She washed her hands, more for want of something to do than anything else and then having counted to a hundred, let herself out of the door.

He was standing in the corridor waiting for her.

'Keith!'

'What's going on?' he asked. He looked hurt, bewildered. She wanted to throw her arms around him and reassure him.

'What are you doing down here, where's your wife?'

'She's gone to the car. I'm supposed to be paying the bill so I can't be a moment. Who's he, the man you're with?'

'I'll explain everything, don't worry,' Felicity said.

'Why didn't you let me know you were back in Cornwall?'

'I don't know,' she said, 'it's complicated. I will ring you, I'll ring you tomorrow.'

'You don't need too,' Keith said. 'I'm behaving like an idiot, I'm sorry, like some stupid love-sick teenager.' Despite herself Felicity smiled and the smile became a laugh. 'What?' said Keith, grinning back despite his anguish.

'I've just been standing in the loo, staring in the mirror and telling myself I'm behaving like some stupid, love-sick teenager.'

'Snap then,' said Keith.

'Yes,' said Felicity. 'Look, you had better go and so had I.'

'Will you call me?'

'I will, I promise.'

The moment of exchanged humour over their stupidity acted like a balm. He clearly thought Simon was a new man in her life, but it would not be difficult to disabuse him. Even in that moment of hurt and misunderstanding they could still laugh. Humour was the cornerstone of their relationship, they were all right. She ran up the stairs and out onto the terrace, head held high ready to enjoy her lunch with Simon.

'So that was her, wasn't it?'

'Who?' Keith asked, making much of starting the engine and putting on his seatbelt.

'I'm not a complete idiot, Keith. That was Felicity Paradise, wasn't it? It's such a stupid name, you couldn't make it up.' Keith began edging the car along the narrow road which led from the café. It was not difficult to give all his concentration to this. Visitors seemed oblivious to the car, pushing buggies in front of it, stepping out just as he was passing.

'Yes, it was Felicity Paradise,' Keith said at last, keeping his eyes firmly on the road.

'So why didn't you introduce us?'

He shrugged.

'I don't know, I suppose it was because she had someone with her.'

'Her new boyfriend by the look of it,' said Barbara with evident satisfaction. 'They were holding hands when they came out onto the terrace.'

'I expect so,' Keith replied, keeping his voice as neutral as possible.

Barbara was not going to let the subject go. 'Still, I don't know why you didn't introduce us, not after all the things that you two have been through. I recognised her from the newspaper reports, though she looked younger than I expected.'

'She's not young,' said Keith, 'only a few years younger than us.'

'Well she doesn't look it, I'll give her that. I wonder why she didn't say hello to you, it all seems very odd to me.'

'I don't think it is,' said Keith. When would this interrogation end? 'As you say, she's obviously got a new man in tow and is a bit shy about it. Perfectly natural I would have thought.'

'Did you see her when you were paying the bill?' said Barbara, with a sudden flash of intuition.

'Briefly,' said Keith; he was a hopeless liar. 'She was on her way to the toilet.'

'The toilets aren't anywhere near the counter where you pay, they're on the opposite side of the room.'

'Oh, for heaven's sake, Barbara, what is this?' Keith began.

'I don't know,' said Barbara, 'you tell me. You have all these adventures with this woman and when finally I clap eyes on her, you don't introduce us. Is there something going on, Keith, is there something I should know?'

'No,' said Keith, at last on safe ground. 'There is nothing going on, Barbara. In all the years that we have been married, I have never looked at another woman, you know that, it's not my style. I couldn't, I wouldn't. Now, can we drop this.'

'So what did she say to you when you saw her?'

'Just hello,' said Keith. 'She's been away, up in Oxford I think. She finds August in St Ives a bit trying. She just told me she was back, that was about it. I was surprised to see her, I thought she was still away.'

'Well she's obviously picked up a new man on her travels.'

'It would appear so,' said Keith, with as little emotion as he could muster.

'Anyway, about this committee meeting this evening. I can leave you something to warm up in the oven or you and Will could go out.' She chattered on. They were back on safe ground. Keith was mightily relieved.

6

They couldn't leave the beach, it was too perfect. The sun blazed down but as the afternoon stretched on there was a slightly autumnal feel to it; it was hot but not too hot. Simon hired a couple of deck-chairs and while he he dozed, Felicity sketched in the notebook she always kept in her handbag; keeping herself busy stopped her from thinking too much about Keith. Around four she went to the beach café and bought two cups of tea and nudging Simon awake, they sat in comfortable silence, drinking their tea.

'I think I'll have another swim,' said Simon.

'This is becoming something of an obsession,' Felicity said. 'You're turning into a real water baby.'

Simon smiled at her. 'I know, it's odd isn't it? I've hardly swum at all since I was a boy. I hate swimming pools and crowds of people. I suppose that's what has put me off. I love the sea though even if it is a bit chilly.'

'Just don't go too far out,' said Felicity, 'you always swim so far – to get away from people I suppose.'

'What are you going to do?'

'I ought to go back and check up on Harvey, he's been stuck inside all afternoon.'

'It's too hot for dogs anyway,' said Simon.

Felicity laughed. 'I don't think you like animals any more than Gilla did.'

'That's not true,' said Simon. 'I'm ambivalent to them, Gilla hated them.'

'Funny isn't it,' said Felicity, 'that someone so positive about everything, is suddenly …' She couldn't go on.

Simon's expression sobered instantly. 'I still can't believe it's happened.'

Felicity shook her head, hot tears springing into her eyes. 'No,' she said, 'we're going through the motions, aren't we, but it doesn't feel real yet.'

Simon stood up and stripped off his t-shirt.

'That's why swimming helps, I think. It clears the mind, sets it free somehow just for a short period.'

'I think I'll ring Ellie before I go back to the house, would you like to speak to her?'

Simon shook his head. 'No, no we spoke last night.'

'Are you sure?' Felicity asked.

'I don't want to crowd her,' he said and started off down the beach.

Felicity watched him go. They had a problem, Simon and Ellie, and somehow she had to help them resolve it. It had to stem from all those years apart – did Ellie resent an absentee father? It was hard to tell. Felicity picked up her mobile and dialled Ellie's number. Ellie answered almost immediately.

'Goodness,' said Felicity, 'you must have almost been sitting on the phone.' Ellie laughed, it was a hollow mirthless laugh. 'Feeling blue?' Felicity asked.

'I am a bit,' she replied, 'in fact I was sitting here wondering whether to telephone you and then I thought I was being rather a bore.'

'Ellie, you've just lost your mother, feeling miserable is normal.'

'I guess,' said Ellie.

'Dad and I are sitting on the beach – well Dad has just gone off for a swim. We had lunch at the Porthminster Beach Café, very spoiling, he insisted, and now he's gone off for his second swim of the day. He's got very keen on swimming, he says it helps to clear his mind.'

'Sounds fun,' said Ellie, bleakly.

'Why don't you come down and join us?' said Felicity. 'The weather is wonderful at the moment. Just take a few days off, please Ellie.'

'No, no,' said Ellie, 'I'm better here, nose to the grindstone and all that.'

'But why?' said Felicity.

'Because,' Ellie hesitated, 'because if I gave in to it, came down to you, I don't think I could go back.'

Felicity was silent for a moment. What Ellie said

made sense but the idea of her suffering alone was appalling. 'That's true,' said Felicity. 'It's a risk. You might find that if you came down here and couldn't face going back, but so what. You could drop out for a year or two, the university would be bound to agree in the circumstances. You're so bright Ellie, you could pick it up anytime you wanted. I'm worried about you.'

'There's no need,' she said, 'I'm fine, I've got some great friends and they've all been marvellous. Last night I went to a concert and tonight I'm having dinner with friends and then we're going clubbing. It's fine, honestly.'

'But will you promise me one thing?' said Felicity. 'If it all gets too much, you won't hesitate, will you? You'll just turn up on my doorstep.'

'Dad's in the spare room at the moment.'

'There's plenty of room for the three of us – the sofa is huge.'

Ellie laughed. 'OK, I promise. Are you going for a swim too? It sounds a lot more appetising than sitting over this pile of books.'

'No, one a day is enough for me.' Felicity shielded her eyes and looked out to sea as she was talking. Simon was swimming strongly, apparently heading for America. She felt an odd note of disquiet – in all his grief he wouldn't do anything silly, would he? No, she dismissed it, of course not – there was Ellie to consider. They chatted for a few more minutes and then agreed to speak later in the week. 'Now you promise me Ellie, promise me you'll call or just arrive?'

'I do,' she said, 'and thanks again for looking after Dad.'

'Bye, darling.'

'Bye, love to Dad.'

Felicity sighed and slipped the mobile into her bag, picked up her sketchbook, collapsed the deckchairs and turned towards the sea once more for a sighting of Simon. For a moment she had difficulty locating him and then she saw him. He was way out, far beyond the other swimmers, but mercifully he seemed to have turned round and was now heading back towards shore. She watched him for a moment or two, for some reason still feeling slightly concerned. Then she put her bag over her shoulder, picked up both the deckchairs and returned them to the café. On the wooden decking outside the café she turned again and stared out to sea. He really was a long way out. There was a small blue and yellow speed boat zig-zagging backwards and forwards between him and the other bathers, which showed just how far he had swum. She stood and watched, uncertain, feeling like an over-protective mother hen. It was ridiculous: he was a big chap and well able to take care of himself.

Suddenly the sound of the speedboat revving its engine echoed across the water, the boat gathered speed and seemed to be heading straight for Simon. 'No,' Felicity shouted. The boat continued on its way.

She heard a thump echoing across the water. It must have made contact with Simon yet she could still see him, his head bobbing about. The boat did not stop but continued on its way heading towards Hayle. Still clutching her bag she ran down towards the shore. She could see another couple of swimmers heading out towards Simon. She stood helplessly on the edge of the shore. He was coming back, the two people with him swimming either side of him. Within a few moments he was on his feet wading out; an elderly man held him up with an arm around his waist, a younger man walked beside him.

'Simon, are you alright?' Felicity cried. 'Oh my God, look at your shoulder.' There was a nasty, livid red gash on his right shoulder, blood was running down his arm, the skin around it already looked mottled and bruised.

'I'm alright,' he said, 'fine, nothing broken. Thanks.' He turned to the older man who detached himself.

'Are you alright, mate?'

'Yeh, I'm fine, honestly.'

'Bloody maniac, what was he at? It looked like he was deliberately trying to run you down,' said the younger man.

'Oh, I don't think so,' said Simon. 'Look if it's OK with everyone, I'm just going to go up the beach and sit down for a few minutes.'

'I'll take you up to hospital,' said Felicity, 'Come

on.' She turned towards the two men, who were clearly father and son. 'Thanks so much for helping him.'

'You should report it to the coastguard. Where did that boat go?' asked the older man, shielding his eyes.

'Towards Hayle,' said Felicity. They all stared out to sea but there was no sign of it now.

'Must have gone like the clappers,' said the younger man. 'Look, our names are Peterson, father and son, we're staying up at the Pedn'Olva Hotel and we're here for another week. If you want to take it any further and need witnesses, we'd be happy to oblige. It's so dangerous these boats messing about amongst the swimmers.'

'In fairness,' said Simon, who had gone very pale and was holding his arm, 'I was out way too far.'

'Come on,' said Felicity, 'we need to get you to the hospital.'

By the time they had walked up from the beach – which was a slow affair being constantly interrupted by various visitors tut-tutting about the danger of speedboats – Simon's colour had returned. 'I don't need to go to the hospital,' he said firmly.

'Yes you do,'said Felicity. 'You need that shoulder x-rayed.'

'I really don't,' he said, 'it's just a bruise and a gash, and it's not deep enough for stitches. Let's just go back to the cottage and I'll lie down for a bit,

83

please. If it hasn't stopped bleeding by the time I get up then I'll go and have it seen to.'

'I don't approve,' said Felicity.

'Tough!' said Simon, with a watery smile.

On their return, Simon took himself off to bed with painkillers and Felicity took an ecstatic Harvey for a walk around the Island. It was a beautiful evening and she and Harvey walked to the end of the pier and sat in the sun, gazing out across the harbour. Most of the cars had left the harbour car park now; it was quiet except for fishermen and the harbour master clearing up after a day's work. The accident with Simon had disturbed her, because in her heart she felt sure it was no accident. It was probably kids messing about, Simon had said, but she had seen the boat coming and it hadn't been kids at the wheel, it was a single man, who could not have failed to see Simon in the water. Clearly he had not meant to do Simon serious damage because he could have killed him, but was it a warning? There was something going on – the lunch with Hugh Randall, the burglary, the bogus reporter who had certainly made no contact and now this – it was all too much of a coincidence and it made her very uneasy.

'Chief Inspector Penrose?'

'Mrs Paradise, good morning, how are you?' Keith's voice sounded warm with welcome.

It was the morning following Simon's accident. Although a little stiff and bruised, he appeared fine and had taken himself off for a walk around the town leaving Felicity free to ring Keith Penrose.

'I'm alright, thanks,' she said, 'well sort of, I have a bit of a problem, actually.'

'Oh Lord,' said Keith, with a theatrical sigh. 'Is this problem going to involve me?'

'I hope so,' said Felicity. 'Are you busy, could I just talk all this through with you?'

'My time is yours,' said Keith, 'hang on a moment.' He got up and walked across his office and shut the door. Then he came and sat down, swivelling his chair around to gaze out over the car park. It was so good to hear from her.

'When I go up to Oxford,' Felicity began, 'I usually stay with my best friend, Gilla.'

'I remember,' said Keith. 'Her daughter is your goddaughter, isn't she?'

'That's it,' said Felicity. 'Well, I went up this time and ...' her voice broke, '... Gilla died,' she managed.

'Died?' said Keith. 'When, how? How awful, I am so sorry.'

Felicity pulled herself together with effort. 'She had a brain haemorrhage, quite suddenly. She collapsed on the floor in the kitchen. I wasn't there, I was on my way home. The man that you saw me with yesterday was her husband, Simon.'

'Oh, I see,' said Keith, hoping his sense of relief

85

was not too evident. 'He's come down to stay with you?'

'Yes,' said Felicity, 'Ellie – that's my goddaughter – and I decided it would probably be best for him and I think it probably is. He's doing a lot of walking and swimming. He has to go back and face life without Gilla sometime, but in these first few weeks I think he's better off down here. It's why I haven't been in touch, Keith. Things have been, well, awful.'

'They must have been. What a dreadful thing to happen!'

'It was but although I owe you an explanation that's not why I rang. You see, I think Simon might be in danger.'

'You haven't had one of your funny turns, have you?' Keith asked.

'No, no, nothing like that.' She told him briefly about Simon's background, his relationship with the bank, the subsequent burglary, the bogus reporter and finally the incident with the boat. When she had finished there was a pause.

'I think it's a bit of a stretch linking the speedboat to the burglary in Oxford.'

'I knew you'd say that,' said Felicity, 'but the driver of the speedboat must have known he'd hit Simon. If it had been a simple accident surely he would have stopped and checked.'

'You'd be amazed at the number of hit and run incidents there are on the roads,' Keith said. There was a silence between them. 'Sorry, sorry,' said Keith, 'just for a moment there I forgot how your husband died, that was an incredibly crass remark, I do apologise.'

'It's OK,' said Felicity. 'I'm sure you're right, I'm sure it's a very human reaction to run away from something you've done which is wrong and Simon had swum way too far. He had definitely strayed from swimming territory into boating territory.'

'You're talking yourself into knots,' said Keith. 'If you're saying it could well have been a legitimate accident why should you think it was anything else?'

'It's you who is tying me up in knots, as usual,' said Felicity. 'The burglary is odd, you must admit. Just searching his study and nothing else, then the reporter that never was, then the accident. It's when you link the three together it looks suspicious.'

'What did Thames Valley say about the burglary?'

'Nothing at all, they weren't interested,' said Felicity. 'They just gave Simon's housekeeper a crime number for insurance purposes but I don't even think there was anything damaged, apart from a window.'

'In fairness to them,' said Keith, 'they can hardly spend any time on a crime that involved nothing more than throwing a few papers around.'

'So there's nothing you can do?' Felicity said.

'Does Simon want to press charges against the speedboat driver, assuming we could find him?'

'No, he absolutely does not, he thinks I'm making a fuss.'

'How ungrateful of him,' Keith said, smiling down the phone.

'Oh stop it,' said Felicity, crossly.

'I am sorry I can't do more to help but I would very much welcome the opportunity of buying you a glass of wine to discuss what can be done to allay your fears. It would be good to see you.' He hoped he did not sound as desperate as he felt.

'That's a very kind offer, Chief Inspector, but just at the moment I've got my hands full with Simon. If I can see an opportunity to sneak out I'll give you a ring.'

'I'm very sorry about your friend, Gilla,' Keith said. 'It must have been a terrible shock.' He was aware he was letting her down, but he could see no way to help.

'It was,' said Felicity, 'still is. Goodbye, Keith.'

They both sat staring at their phones having replaced the receivers, both feeling unhappy with the conversation. It had been awkward and slightly tetchy and so much had been left unsaid.

7

15 September 2008, St Ives, Cornwall

The opportunity to see Keith Penrose came sooner than Felicity had expected, in fact just four days later. After a late night supper at Caffé Pasta and a wonderful midnight walk along the beach with Harvey, she was late rising to find Simon already up and dressed, television blaring and newspapers spread out all over the kitchen table.

'Goodness, what's going on?' Felicity asked.

'I just can't believe it,' Simon replied, 'I can't believe they let it go.'

'Who let what go?' Felicity said, frowning over the kettle.

'Lehman Brothers, they've collapsed and the American government hasn't stepped in to save them.'

Felicity poured boiling water into the teapot, silent for a moment. 'This financial crisis that seems to be building around the world is serious, isn't it, Simon?'

Simon nodded. 'It's the by-product of being so able to communicate globally. It's good on the one hand when things are booming but when something goes wrong, it spreads like wildfire. I just can't believe they didn't bail it out, Lehman Brothers, it's madness to let it go.'

'So how does Lehman's collapse affect things?' Felicity frowned. 'Sorry Simon, you couldn't just turn the television down a bit, could you, I can't hear myself think.'

'Yes, of course, sorry.' He reached for the remote and lowered the volume.

'If the Americans haven't bailed out Lehmans does that mean our government won't bail out Carlyon?'

'I honestly don't know,' Simon replied. 'There is nothing in the press about Carlyon. There are rumblings about Lloyds and HBOS and the Royal Bank of Scotland seem to be in trouble too, but there's not a whisper about Carlyon.'

'Maybe they've already got their government bail-out.'

Simon shook his head. 'No, they couldn't have done, not without it being in the press. The Government can't start pledging taxpayers' money on that scale without making it public knowledge. That would be impossible.'

'So your mate, Hugh Randall, must be a nervous man this morning,' Felicity suggested, 'wondering if the Government will play copy cat with Carlyon.'

'I suppose so,' said Simon, his eyes on the screen. 'Look, it's unreal.'

Felicity looked up at the television. A stream of young people were pouring out of the Lehman Brothers offices in the City, cardboard boxes under their arms containing the contents of their desks.

'A lot of them will never find another job in banking, there just won't be enough to go around,' Simon said, 'their careers over before they're hardly started.'

'That's awful,' said Felicity, 'they look absolutely shell-shocked.'

'I've been wondering,' said Simon, 'would you mind if I just hung around the house today? I'd like to make a few phone calls to old colleagues, find out what's going on.'

Felicity smiled at him. Despite Gilla's best efforts to involve him in her somewhat wacky and eccentric life, he was still a banker at heart. 'No problem,' she said, an idea already forming in her mind. 'I might go out this morning and come back after lunch. Would that be OK?'

Simon nodded, his concentration back on the television.

Felicity took her tea back to her bedroom and having dressed, telephoned Keith Penrose.

'I am free for lunch if it's an early one, I've got an appointment at two,' he said.

'Heron at Malpas, it's a beautiful day,' Felicity said.

'See you there. Would twelve be OK?'

Felicity walked past a totally absorbed Simon, collected Harvey and left the house. Having given Harvey a quick run on the beach, she decided to drive straight to Malpas and walk him again after lunch. Once in the car she allowed her mind to drift away from Simon, Gilla, Ellie and Lehman Brothers and think about her forthcoming meeting with Keith Penrose. They had not seen one another properly for over three months and she had missed him terribly. However, she felt considerably calmer about meeting him than she had done before leaving so hurriedly for Oxford. There was no future for their relationship, except as friends, but good friends were to be valued, treasured and true friends were hard to come by. Keith Penrose was a true friend and it was enough. At last she felt she was ready to accept that. She was used to widowhood now, enjoyed her freedom even, had no problem at all about being alone, particularly now she had Harvey for company. With her daughter just down the road and a new baby arriving any moment there was plenty to absorb her. Even if the opportunity of a man in her life presented itself, she was not sure she would welcome it now. She had been happily married for many years, raised two children, been seemingly secure in the hub of family life … but nothing in life stays the same and that stage was over. She thought back to the conversation she'd had with Gilla when she had confessed her feelings for Keith Penrose. It seemed like a lifetime away. Gilla's death had changed everything – things that had seemed so desperately important no longer did so. Life had a different sort of perspective, the shock and misery of losing her best friend had made her oddly calmer. She could look forward to meeting Keith as a dear friend, with no nerves or doubts or regrets. Seeing him with his wife had brought home to her the reality of the situation and she was fine with that, she realised.

Keith Penrose by contrast was not at all calm. On replacing the receiver from Felicity's call, he ran a hand around his jaw wondering whether he had shaved properly that morning. He was wearing his old suit and a rather crumpled rugby club tie – it was not a good look, he thought with a slight smile. God, he was pathetic. The thought of seeing her again after all these weeks was so … he shook his head trying to find the words to explain to himself how he felt about Felicity Paradise and failed. He was not used to these huge swings of emotion, it was not how Keith Penrose worked. While always a compassionate man, good with people of all ages, his own feelings concerning close relationships had been steady as a rock and very much under control until now.

Harvey broke the ice by running across the terrace and hurling himself at Keith's legs, wagging his tail ecstatically.

'Well, someone's pleased to see me,' said Keith.

'We both are,' said Felicity, coming up to him. Keith straightened up from patting the dog and she leaned forward and kissed him briefly on the cheek.

'It's been a long while,' said Keith, staring at her. 'At least it feels like it. You're looking good.' And she was, her still-fair hair bleached by the sun, a light tan and as usual eccentrically dressed in jeans, stripy top and mad quirky purple boots.

'You too,' she said, meaning it. There was an awkward silence between them.

'Shall we go and get some food and then we can settle down?'

'You do it,' said Felicity, 'I'll bag a table on the terrace while there's still one left. I don't mind what I have.'

He reappeared a few moments later carrying two glasses of wine. 'I've ordered a crab salad, is that alright?'

'Perfect,' she answered. They sat at a table in the sun overlooking the estuary and raised glasses to one another.

'I wasn't expecting to see you so soon,' he said.

'We have Lehman Brothers to thank for that,'

said Felicity. 'Simon was so absorbed in their collapse, he didn't need babysitting today.'

'It is terrible,' said Keith, 'I just wonder where all this financial mayhem is going to end?'

'It's scary,' Felicity agreed, 'particularly as I don't really understand it, well actually I don't understand it at all.'

'I'm just glad my children seem to be settled into safe careers, assuming anything's safe. Your boy is in IT, isn't he?' Keith asked.

'Yes, he's a consultant, he has his own business. He would be absolutely hopeless at it but for his wife. I mean he's a genius and all that but he'd never remember to bill people. She runs the business side and he just does all the clever fiddling about.'

Keith laughed. 'I don't think he'd thank you for describing his life's work as fiddling about.'

'You know what I mean,' said Felicity. 'And how is Will doing?'

'Good,' said Keith. 'He's buckled down to his course and still living at home – well he can't do anything else really, he hasn't any money. It's hard for him after the independence of the Army but on the whole, he is doing really well. He and Barbara have the odd flare-up, of course.'

'That was embarrassing, wasn't it,' said Felicity, 'when we met at the Porthminster?'

Keith nodded. 'I didn't know what to do. I was taken aback by you being with Simon. I shouldn't have been, of course, but I was and I didn't know how to deal with it. So, of course, being me, I did nothing.' He hesitated. 'Barbara realised who you were.'

'Did she, how?' said Felicity.

'From the newspapers. Some of our exploits have produced a fair amount of press coverage, haven't they, over the years?'

'I suppose so. Did she think it was odd that we didn't speak or make introductions?'

'Very,' said Keith, 'I had some explaining to do.'

'What did you say?'

'Well, nothing much, I sort of bluffed my way out of it.'

'Would you rather we didn't meet any more,' Felicity asked, 'if it's awkward for you?'

The look of abject misery that crossed his face was so moving that for a moment Felicity turned away, squinting into the sun. The pain she saw there shocked her to the core.

'No,' said Keith, after a moment, 'no, of course not.'

'Only,' Felicity replied, 'I don't want to make things awkward for you.'

'It's not awkward,' Keith said, his voice gruff with emotion. 'I don't think I could bear it if we didn't see each other, ever.'

Felicity turned to look at him. 'You do recognise that all we're ever going to be is friends, Keith?'

'Absolutely,' he said.

'Well then, let's drink to friendship,' she said, lightening the mood. They chinked glasses and smiled at one another; they were back on safe ground. Conversation flowed through lunch around family and children and their coffee was drunk and their bill paid by the time they returned to the subject of Simon and the financial crisis that seemed to be developing around the world. 'They say we're in for the biggest and deepest recession ever,' Felicity said.

'Nothing new to West Cornwall,' said Keith, with a smile, 'we're always in recession except in August.'

Felicity laughed. 'That's true, isn't it? I think we've got one of the lowest standards of living in Europe.'

Keith shrugged and stood up. Reaching for his jacket, he expansively swept his arm in the direction of the estuary laid out before them. 'That may be true but I couldn't live anywhere else. Could you... now?'

Felicity shook her head. 'No, no I don't think I could.'

'Come on, I'll walk you to your car.'

They walked down the steps from the terrace and Keith took her arm; it was warm, companionable, easy and comforting.

'So, no more dramas, imagined or otherwise, with your friend Simon, no more attempts on his life?' Keith was laughing at her, one eyebrow raised.

'You may mock Chief Inspector, but something

isn't right. People will do anything where there is money involved, particularly big money like this. I am worried and I'm right to be. You can smile all you like but I'm keeping a very close eye on him.'

'This bank he was involved in, are they going to go bust like Lehmans?' Keith asked.

Felicity shrugged. 'He doesn't know, there was nothing in the press about them at all at the moment, which is odd because he knows they're in trouble.'

'Obviously there are forces at work behind the scenes.'

'Obviously,' said Felicity, 'and that's what worries me because they know Simon has the power to mess things up.'

'I think you might be accused of being a touch melodramatic there, Mrs Paradise.'

'Well for once, Chief Inspector, I just hope you're right.'

'Take comfort from the fact, Mrs Paradise, that you have the full might of Devon and Cornwall Constabulary at your disposal should anything go wrong.'

'Most reassuring,' said Felicity, with a smile.

Whenever Felicity found herself in Malpas, she always stopped at the playing fields just short of town and walked over to the estuary bank to pay homage and remember the life of a very sad woman. Lizzie Hope, wife to Philip, mother to Megan and George, had been pulled out of the Fal Estuary three years before, having been strangled by her lover. Lizzie was a alcoholic. Lizzie's was an Oxfordshire family like Felicity's own and they had met but once, and fatefully. Felicity had been at the school gates of the Oxford prep school where she worked. That day she was the member of staff in charge of children leaving the school and she had failed to stop drunken Lizzie from loading her children into her car. Ten minutes later on the Oxford ring road, Lizzie had crashed her car, killing her daughter Megan. It was an incident that had haunted Felicity for years, and still did. It was something she knew she would never be free of, the knowledge that she should have done more to stop Lizzie. She was still in touch with the family – George, the surviving child, had been adopted by his grandparents. They spoke regularly on the phone and occasionally Felicity visited. George was doing well and she was certain that Lizzie's parents bore her no grudge. Still, though, she knew that her split second of indecision had cost Megan her life and it was a tough thing to live with.

Despite lunch with Keith and the beautiful weather, thoughts of Lizzie Hope had dampened Felicity's spirits, as she walked down from Barnoon car park to her cottage. She climbed the stairs to her kitchen feeling suddenly weary, relieved that there was no sound from upstairs, suggesting that Simon was out walking or swimming, as usual. In fact, he was sitting on the balcony staring out across the harbour.

He turned his head as she came in. He looked awful. 'Hello Fizzy.'

'Simon, what's wrong, you look white as a sheet?'

'I've just had a bit of a shock, that's all.'

Felicity came out onto the balcony to join him, pulling up a chair next to him. 'Why, what's happened?'

'It's Alex Button, the chap I told you about, the one in Hong Kong who was making inappropriate investments.'

'What about him?' Felicity asked.

'He's dead, he was shot two days ago.'

'Oh my God,' said Felicity, 'how did you hear, how did you find out?'

'I was messing about online, scrolling through any news I could glean on the subject of Carlyon, obviously trying to find out where they stood in view of the Lehman Brothers collapse. I just picked up this news item that a former employee of Carlyon had been found shot dead in Hong Kong.'

'A former employee, so he'd left the bank?'

'Yes, I hadn't realised that. He was fired about a week before Hugh had lunch with me. He never mentioned it.'

'So was it suicide then?' Felicity asked.

'That's what I immediately assumed but apparently not – he was murdered. I didn't think there was much point in ringing the Bank direct, I knew they would tell me nothing but I still have a good friend out in Hong Kong, a lawyer. I telephoned him and he told me all about it – apparently it's been the talk of the town. Alex was found with a bullet in the back of his head in an alleyway in the red light district of Hong Kong. He appeared to have been drinking heavily and he was carrying enough cocaine to party for several years.'

'So his death had nothing to do with the bank then?' Felicity asked.

'That's how it was meant to look, but …' Simon hesitated.

'But what?' said Felicity.

'Alex was an odd sort of character, absolutely committed to his job, it was his life. He wasn't married, never seemed to have any girlfriends – or boyfriends come to that. He was a rather colourless person, without a great deal of identifiable character or personality. There was one thing about him though.'

'What was that?' Felicity asked.

'He didn't drink and he certainly would never have done drugs.'

'Perhaps being sacked tipped him over.'

'I very much doubt it,' said Simon.

'So what does the "talk of the town" say then, what does your lawyer friend think, and come to that, what do the Hong Kong police have to say about it?'

'My friend, Ben Brown, says the rumours flying around are that Alex Button was a danger to the Bank. Whether he had threatened to go the press or tell tales to the FSA I don't know, but Ben's view is that he was murdered because he knew too much. Everyone knows that Carlyon is in trouble and desperately trying to find a bail-out package. In Hong Kong at any rate, it is generally believed that Alex Button was a potential whistle-blower so they took him out. Nothing will ever be proved, of course, at least that's Ben's view.'

'Oh, my God,' said Felicity. 'You're a potential whistle-blower, Simon.'

'I don't think I'm much of a risk,' said Simon, sounding far from convinced. 'Hugh warned me off and he's no reason to assume I won't keep my mouth shut. If it's true that Alex was killed because he was a potential threat to the Bank's future, his information would be current and much more damaging than anything I could say now. If I had wanted to have any real impact, I should have gone to the FSA when I submitted my report and Hugh sacked me. I knew what I was talking about then but I've no idea what Carlyon have been up to in the last couple of years. I'm no danger now and they know it.'

'I disagree,' said Felicity. 'I know absolutely nothing about banking but it seems to me that when you highlighted the Bank's problems – even if it was over two years ago – the Chairman chose to ignore you and continued to trade inappropriately. This leaves you in a position to demonstrate that the directors have been criminally negligent or even fraudulent in continuing to trade knowing the problems they had, assuming of course that Hugh shared his knowledge with the rest of the board.'

'But if I've kept quiet since my pay-off, why should I suddenly start causing trouble now?'

'Because the bank is in trouble,' said Felicity, patiently. 'Whoever bails it out – if anyone bails it out – they should be made aware that the current board is not to be trusted and you might feel it your duty to say so.' There was a lengthy silence between them. 'So are we going to talk about the speedboat incident the other day or are we going to ignore that too?'

'That was probably just an accident,' Simon said, firmly.

'Oh yes,' said Felicity. 'I was there, Simon, the guy was deliberately trying to mow you down.'

'If the guy was trying to kill me, he didn't make a very good job of it. I think it was just a stupid accident.'

'Or maybe he wasn't that experienced with boats, there was quite a swell that day, and he planned to kill you but messed up. God, Simon you could have been shot like poor Alex Button. So far from the beach, it would have been ages before anyone realised what had happened.'

'Oh come on Fizzy, I think you're getting carried

away.'

'Am I? You've been warned off by the Chairman, you've had your flat raided, you've been run down by a speedboat and now you hear that a former colleague has been shot dead. Isn't it about time we took this seriously?'

'You don't have to worry about me,' said Simon, 'I'll be alright.'

'Actually,' said Felicity. 'I wasn't worrying about you, not at all.'

'Oh, thanks a bunch,' said Simon, his anger flaring to match Felicity's.

Felicity stood up. 'I'm not worrying about you, Simon, because I'm worrying far more about Ellie. Ellie has already lost one parent, she doesn't need to lose another.'

Supper was a tense affair. Felicity made them omelettes and salad but neither of them was hungry and both preoccupied. At last over coffee Felicity raised the subject again. 'So, since you're living in my house, Simon, are you going to confide in me as to what you're planning to do about all this?'

'If you feel I'm a threat to you in any way, by being here, I'll go back to Oxford of course.'

Felicity laid a hand on his arm. 'You know that's not what I'm saying, but I am worried and I think I'm right to be. I agree Alex Button probably made some threats whereas you've made none but until Carlyon has found its backer, I do think we need to be very careful and vigilant and you need to keep a very low profile.'

'The alternative is to blow the whistle on them without any prior threats, just go directly to the FSA, and then lie low. With the deed done, the threat I pose is exposed and the whole thing is over.'

'But why Simon, why put yourself in any danger? You've just lost your wife, your daughter needs you and this is not your problem. When you worked for the Bank you advised the Chairman that you thought there were some dirty tricks going on and by doing so, you did your duty. He chose to ignore you but that's his problem not yours. Step away from it, leave it behind, think of the future, there is no point in dwelling on the past.'

'I don't have a future,' said Simon, 'not without Gilla.'

'You have a daughter,' Felicity thundered, 'so you make damn sure you have a future. Gilla would be appalled to think you were not putting Ellie ahead of every other consideration.' Simon and Felicity were glaring at one another, the atmosphere in the room crackling with tension. At that moment the phone rang. Felicity jumped up, relieved to have something to do.

'Fizzy, it's Martin. We're off, Mel's in labour. Could you possibly come over and look after Minty? I need to get Mel to hospital right now. I don't think

105

this one is going to take very long.'

'Oh Martin,' said Felicity, 'how exciting! How is she, is she in a lot of pain?'

'The contractions are pretty strong.'

'I'll be right over,' said Felicity. 'Five minutes and I'll be packed up and ready to go.'

'Bring Simon too, if you want to.'

'Thanks,' said Felicity. She replaced the receiver. 'Mel's gone into labour. I must go over and look after Minty. Do you want to come too?'

Simon shook his head. 'No, it's a family time, I'll stay here.'

'Will you be alright?'

'Of course I'll be alright.'

Felicity headed for the door and hesitated. 'You won't do anything stupid will you, Simon?'

'No, no I won't,' said Simon. 'And don't think I'm not aware of my responsibilities to Ellie, it's just that …'

'There is no just,' Felicity cut in angrily. 'You men are all the same. I know you're not the sort of chap who would wish Alex Button dead, but you're finding this whole thing quite exciting, enjoying the drama – what's going to happen to the Bank, who knows what, who will tell what to whom – I'm glad that it's taking your mind off Gilla but just stay out of the fray – please.'

8

Charles Robert Tregonning was born at 5.16 a.m. the following morning, a healthy contented baby with a definite look of the grandfather after whom he was named. By lunchtime Mel was home and Martin, Mel, Felicity and Minty crowded round the carrycot gazing in awe at their new family member. His tuft of hair was fair to the point of being almost white, his eyes when he briefly opened them, were a startling blue, his grandfather's colouring.

'Dad would be so proud,' Felicity said, her voice trembling.

Mel took her hand and squeezed it. 'Are you happy for him to be called after Dad?'

'Of course I am. Will he be known as Charlie?'

'Absolutely,' said Martin. 'Look at him, it's the perfect name for him.' And indeed it was.

Felicity prepared lunch and as soon as it was eaten, Mel and Charlie were dispatched to bed.

'I'll stay on for a few days, shall I?' said Felicity, as

she and Martin were washing up.

'It would be great, if you don't mind,' said Martin. 'The gardens are quietening down now as the season is coming to an end so I can be around if you feel you can't stay.'

'I'd love to,' said Felicity, 'if I'm not going to be in the way?'

'I don't know how we'd manage without you, and Harvey,' he added, smiling fondly at Minty who was sitting on the battered old sofa in the kitchen cuddling Harvey, who clearly adored her. 'What about Simon, though, and Ellie come to that?'

'Ellie was planning to stay in Edinburgh for the time being and I think Simon will be fine about me staying with you for a few days.' Felicity dropped her voice to just above a whisper. 'To give you and Mel and Charlie a bit of bonding time, why don't I take Minty to collect some of my things? I literally brought only my toothbrush last night. We could have a play on the beach and then I can talk the whole thing through with Simon and see what he wants to do. In my view, he'll be quite happy to spend a few days on his own at the cottage and maybe with my room empty it would be a good opportunity for him to persuade Ellie to come down for the weekend.'

'If you're sure that's alright,' said Martin.

'I think it's going to have to be,' said Felicity, briskly. 'I was thinking about it overnight. Simon is a grown man and I have nannied him for over three weeks now. It might be a good idea for him to face some of his demons while he's still down here in Cornwall. It's going to be really tough for him going back to the family home so being on his own for a while could be a good halfway house. I'm happy to have him but he can't stay with me forever.'

Martin grinned at her. 'Put like that, we're positively doing poor old Simon a favour then by dragging you away from him.'

'Absolutely.' She walked over to the sofa and scooped Minty up into her arms. 'What about coming to St Ives with me, we'll have a play on the beach and then I can collect some things because I'm going to come and stay with you for a few days, if that's OK?'

'Granny, Granny,' Minty said, throwing her arms around Felicity's neck.

Felicity smiled at Martin over the top of Minty's head. 'And it's not just Simon who would benefit from me being here for a few days,' she said, 'I will absolutely love it.'

Felicity decided they should go to Bamaluz Beach because dogs were allowed on it and it was sheltered from what was proving to be a nasty sharp little wind. Autumn was definitely upon them and she shivered as she sat on a rock watching Minty and Harvey running backwards and forwards across the sand in pursuit of a mini-football. It was when she was alone like this, in happy circumstances, that the awfulness of Gilla's death haunted her. The simple pleasure of sitting by the sea watching your grandchild and dog mess about, the beauty of the day, these were things which Gilla would never enjoy, she would never know what it was to have a grandchild. She was missing so much and so by definition was Felicity, the loss of a lifetime's friendship. They were supposed to grow old together, they had promised to share a room together in an old people's home when their time came, smuggling in bottles of sherry – Gilla's idea of course. There was no one left in the world who knew her as Gilla had, nor ever would. Tears pricked her eyes and she brushed them away hurriedly. Minty with the natural instinct of the very young ran over to her.

'Are you OK Gran?'

'Fine,' said Felicity. 'You two are having fun. Five more minutes and we'll go back to the cottage. You're wet through, just as well I bought a change of clothes.'

Half an hour later Felicity trailed an exhausted Minty up the lane to her cottage. All three of them were wet and covered in sand and, not for the first time, Felicity wished she had a garden or a courtyard or even an efficient wetroom which could play host to the excesses of living in a town dominated by beaches. Once little Charlie has found his feet my house is going to be knee-deep in sand, Felicity thought, not without pleasure.

She opened the front door and picking Minty up

carried her straight through to the bathroom. 'Simon,' she called up the stairs, 'are you there?' She was greeted by silence. Minty and Harvey showered together which proved to be an extremely messy affair. She wrapped Minty in a towel, found her a drink and a biscuit and turned on children's television. Time for a quick shower herself and packing and then they needed to be off. They had spent much longer on the beach than Felicity had intended and she wanted to be back in good time for Minty's bedtime. Mel did not like her routines disturbed as Felicity knew to her cost.

Felicity gazed around the room. The kitchen was tidy except for a half drunk mug of coffee on the kitchen table and *The Times* opened at the crossword. Simon's fountain pen lay on the paper and Felicity absentmindedly picked it up and screwed on the cap. She wandered out to the balcony. There was no sign of life there, so she shut the French windows in order to keep the kitchen warm for Minty. It took a while to get ready to leave and a tired Minty was uncooperative about being dressed and had to be bribed with a second biscuit. Then, predictably, Mel rang wanting to know where they were.

'It's her brother's very first day,' Mel said, 'Minty should be here with him.'

'I'm sorry,' said Felicity, 'I didn't mean this to go on so long but she was having such fun on the beach with Harvey. I won't be longer than half an hour, I promise.'

'By the time you get here it will be time for her to go to bed,' Mel complained.

At last they were ready, Harvey fed, Minty dressed, herself packed but still having to face the endless steps up to Barnoon. She knew she was taking her time because she was hoping Simon would appear and help her up to the car park, but there was no sign of him. She scrawled a quick note saying she would be staying another day or two at Mel's and would ring him later, then clutching a protesting Minty by one hand and the suitcase and Harvey's lead in the other, she began the long ascent to the car park.

The evening sped by. Mel and Minty were tired and bad-tempered and there was tea to get for Minty and supper for the adults, the washing machine was in constant use and so it was nearly ten o'clock by the time Felicity remembered that she had not rung Simon. She dialled her home number but there was still no reply.

'That's odd,' she said to Martin over her shoulder, 'I'd have thought he'd have been home by now.'

'By all accounts he's been wining and dining you for weeks so he has probably acquired a taste for it. I expect he's simply gone out to eat.'

'Yes,' said Felicity, 'but you'd think on his own

he'd probably eat early, wouldn't you?'

'I don't know, maybe he met someone and went on to the pub or something. He's a big boy, he'll be alright, Fizzy, don't worry.'

'I'll just try his mobile.' She rang his mobile but it went straight to answerphone.

'Well that's not surprising,' Martin reassured her, 'there are plenty of places in St Ives where you can't get a signal.'

'I suppose so,' Felicity frowned. 'I'll leave it for tonight but I'll give him a ring very early tomorrow morning.'

'And I don't think you'll need an alarm clock to wake you up early tomorrow, do you?'

'I should imagine not,' Felicity said, with a smile.

As predicted, by six the following morning Felicity had Minty in her bed and was reading her stories. By seven she felt she was justified in ringing Simon. Again the phone rang out and was unanswered; again she tried his mobile which went straight to answerphone. Something wasn't right, she felt sure of it but she forced herself to be cheerful during breakfast as she made the family scrambled eggs.

'So does anybody need anything doing today?' Martin asked. 'I should pop into the garden for an hour or two and I can do a shop on the way back. Will you girls be staying here?'

'I hope you'll be here today, Mum,' said Mel, a

little pointedly.

'I will, of course,' Felicity began.

'But,' said Mel, picking up on the hesitation.

'But I am worried about Simon. He wasn't there when I went over yesterday, I rang him last night and I rang again this morning and there is still no reply.'

'Oh, for heaven's sake Mum, he's a grown man! He's well able to look after himself.'

Felicity smiled at her daughter. 'That's what your husband said, but I am concerned about him. Understandably he's been in a very funny state since Gilla died. Would you mind if I just dashed over to St Ives and tried to track him down?'

'So what are you going to do, tour the bars, scour the beaches?' Mel asked, scornfully.

'No, no nothing so complicated or time-consuming. If he's not at home I'll pop down and see Annie and get her to keep an eye out for him – no one escapes Annie's clutches for long. I just feel a bit uneasy about him.'

'You don't think he's the suicidal type, do you?' Martin asked.

'No, no I don't, he has Ellie to think about apart from anything else. It's just,' she hesitated. 'I'm sworn to secrecy so I can't go into details but the bank he used to work for is in trouble apparently and Simon has some information that could do them harm, if he disclosed the details. I'm just worried they might have …'

'Oh Mum, for heaven's sake, trust you to create

a drama where none exists.' Mel was clearly exasperated.

Felicity looked crestfallen. 'I tell you what,' said Martin. 'I'll ring the Gardens now and say I'll be in later. Why don't you pop over to St Ives right away and see if there is any sign of Simon while I wait here with Mel and the children until you get back.'

Felicity gave him a look of gratitude. 'Thanks,' she said, 'I'll be as quick as I can, honestly.'

He was not at the cottage. During the drive from Hayle, Felicity had convinced herself that he had simply been in the shower and not heard the phone and that she would walk in to find him brewing coffee and frying bacon. On calling his name, however, she was greeted with the same silence as on the previous day. She had climbed the stairs to the kitchen. The French windows were still shut and the air a little musty. She threw open the windows and turned around to study the kitchen. The sight that greeted her was not reassuring. Still on the table was the coffee cup, the paper and Simon's pen exactly where she had left it the previous evening. He hasn't been back here, Felicity thought. She ran downstairs and into the spare room. The bed was made, man-fashion, his clothes, suitcase, shaving gear were spread around the room.

'Laptop,' she said aloud. She scoured around the room, under the bed – no sign of it. She looked in the little wardrobe – nothing; bedside table – no. She ran upstairs again and looked around the sitting room and the kitchen hurriedly and then went out onto the balcony in case she had missed something – there was no laptop. Phone – she repeated the same exercise again and added it to the roll call; his phone was missing and so was his laptop. She sat down at the kitchen table and thought for a few moments, then reaching for her mobile, she called Simon and Gilla's Oxford home. There was no reply. Searching through her list of received calls, she found June's number and telephoned. On the second ring it picked up.

'June, hello, it's Felicity Paradise.'

'Oh, hello,' said June, 'how are things? How is Mr Carter doing?'

'Fine,' said Felicity, 'only I've mislaid him. I've been away for a couple of nights and I've just got back home and he's not here. He hasn't come back up to Oxford, has he?'

'No, bless you. I've just got back from the house – all is well there incidentally, no more trouble – but there is certainly no sign of Mr Carter. Were you expecting him back up here?'

'No, not really,' said Felicity, 'it was just a long shot. I expect he's just gone for a walk or something, only ...'

'Only what?' said June, immediately picking up something was wrong. 'Are you worried about him?'

'No, not at all,' said Felicity, 'I'm sorry to have

116

troubled you, June.'

'Would you like me to check the house again later, see if he's back, have you tried his mobile?'

'I have,' said Felicity, 'he's not picking up at the moment, but yes, that would be good. You have my number, don't you?'

'Yes,' said June, 'I'll call you later. I'll pop in again after lunch.'

More difficult was the telephone call to Ellie. Ellie sounded a bit bleak.

'How are you getting on?' Felicity asked.

'Oh, the work's piling up.'

'Are you finding it hard?'

'I am a bit, Fizz,' Ellie admitted. 'I'm finding my concentration is not all that great. I start work and then I suddenly go off at a tangent and then start thinking, well you know, about Mum and stuff.'

'Have you talked to your tutor about it?'

'No,' said Ellie, 'and I don't want to especially.'

'Would you like me to?'

'No, no don't make a fuss, I'll be alright, it's just I've always been rather good at studying and now I find I'm not.'

'It's very early days, Ellie. I do think you should tell someone about your difficulties so they can give you more time, more leeway.'

'But I don't want that,' said Ellie, 'I need to be stretched and that way I don't have time to think.'

'Have you heard from Dad?' Felicity asked,

casually.

'No, not for several days, I keep meaning to ring him but to be honest, Fizzy, I don't know what to say to him.'

'What does he say to you?'

'Not much, that's the trouble. We've never been great communicators, he and I, as you know we have always operated through Mum, and now there's no Mum we've just got nothing to say to each other. It's sad but I don't know how to break through.'

'I was going to suggest you came down this weekend. I'm staying over at Mel's at the moment.' Felicity went on to explain about the birth of Charlie to squeals of delight from Ellie.

'That's so cool, I'm so pleased for you. I'd love to come down and see the baby; I could come this weekend.'

'OK, I'll tell Dad when I see him.'

'And how is he?'

'He's fine,' Felicity lied fluently.

'Good-oh, well send him my love then. I'd better go, I have to meet a friend for a coffee.'

So he wasn't in Oxford, he hadn't contacted his daughter, he hadn't been in the cottage overnight – where was he? Felicity felt chilled and anxious, something wasn't right. Her immediate instinct was to ring Keith but she knew she was going to have trouble persuading him to take her seriously. 'I'll go and see Annie,' she thought.

Cormorant Cottage was as warm and welcoming as ever and from nowhere, it seemed, Annie produced warm drop scones, a large cup of tea, a pat of butter and some homemade blackberry jam.

'You sit down, my girl, and tell me what's up – you look all in.'

'I don't think I could eat anything, thank you Annie, I feel a bit queasy actually.'

'All the more reason to have a scone, come on now.'

Felicity took a bite and of course, they were so delicious, she found that she was hungry and that eating something helped.

'Proper job,' said Annie, approvingly. 'Now tell me what's going on. Something is wrong, I can see that. Tell me about poor little Ellie, how is she bearing up?'

Felicity had telephoned Annie from Oxford to tell her of Gilla's death but they had barely seen one another since Felicity had returned to St Ives, such had been the extent of her involvement with Simon.

'She's not doing too bad,' said Felicity, sipping her mug of tea. 'I spoke to her just now actually, she's having difficulty concentrating on her studies.'

'Of course she is, poor little pet. I think she's very brave to be going back to university at all. She should be down here with you and her dad.'

'I suppose you're right,' said Felicity, 'and yet I can see where she is coming from – she wants to keep her life on track and stay as normal as possible.'

'But it's not normal,' Annie said, 'losing your mum. I think you should be some firm with her, tell her to forget her work for a minute. The university would let her do that, wouldn't they?'

'I should think so, Annie, in the circumstances. Anyway, she is coming down to St Ives the weekend after next so I'll throw her to you and see what you can do to sort her out.'

'Poor little maid, she doesn't need old Annie giving her a hard time as well as everything else.'

'She's very fond of you,' Felicity said.

'And I her, I've been thinking about her a lot recently.'

Felicity placed her hand on Annie's arm. 'You're not a bad old thing, are you really?'

'You're a cheeky maid,' said Annie, her little bird-like face breaking into a grin.

'Anyway,' said Felicity, 'before I tell you why I'm here I've got some very exciting news for you.' She paused, theatrically. 'Mel's had her baby.'

Annie clapped her hands together in delight. 'Oh, what's she got?'

'A little boy, she's named him Charlie after my …'

'After your husband,' Annie finished for her. 'That's lovely, she's got a good heart has Mel. She can be a bit teasy at times, but she's as good as gold underneath it all. Is she well, and the baby?'

'They're both fine,' said Felicity, 'in fact, I shouldn't be here now, I'm supposed to be on duty.'

'I don't know how you can tear yourself away,' said Annie, 'I love them when they're very newborn. I know a lot of people prefer babies when they're sitting up and taking notice but I love them when they're brand new – that smell! Do you think Mel would mind if I got one of my boys to run me over to see her and the baby?'

'Of course she wouldn't, you know how fond she is of you but I tell you what, you don't need to bother one of your boys, I'll bring you over there. How about tomorrow or the next day? Just depending on how she is, her milk is coming in so she might be a bit teary.'

'That would be marvellous,' said Annie, leaning forward and refilling Felicity's mug. 'Now what about another scone?'

'No, really Annie, thanks. Apart from anything else I must get back but I wondered if I could ask you a favour.'

'That's usually why you come round here,' said Annie, 'wanting something.'

'Not true,' Felicity protested.

'As true as I live and breathe,' said Annie, 'so what can I do for you?'

Felicity bit her lip and looked pensively at Annie. 'Simon has gone missing,' she said.

'What do you mean, gone missing?' Annie asked sharply.

'Well, I don't know exactly,' said Felicity. She recounted the events of the previous twenty-four hours. 'So you can imagine when I got back to the cottage this morning and found everything exactly as it was, I started to panic.'

'You don't think he's the sort who would top himself, do you?' Annie asked, bluntly.

'No, I don't,' said Felicity, 'he has his black moments but he's not doing too badly. He's loving being in St Ives walking and swimming. He's eating properly, apparently sleeping not too badly and just yesterday he was taking a real interest in the banking crisis. You know he's a banker, or at least he was?'

Annie nodded.

'Studying the papers, searching the internet, he certainly hasn't been sitting around staring at a blank wall. Besides there's Ellie, he would have to be a very self-centred, disturbed person to put Ellie in the position of losing both parents.'

'I hear what you say, my bird, but then if he hasn't topped himself what is he up to?' Annie asked.

'I know you'll think I'm mad Annie, but I'm frightened somebody may have kidnapped him.'

'Oh Lordy, Lordy,' said Annie, 'here we go again, one of Felicity Paradise's little dramas. Why on earth should anybody kidnap Simon in St Ives?'

'Well,' said Felicity, 'the bank he used to work

for is in trouble and Simon has inside information which would expose that the directors had known for some time that the Bank was insolvent and had done nothing to rectify it. The Bank is hoping for a bail-out and I reckon that they reckon that Simon could scupper the deal. Does that make sense?'

'Makes sense, I suppose,' said Annie, grudgingly, 'but sounds a bit far-fetched to me. So you reckon somebody has come down from the Bank, put a hood over Simon's head, whisked him off and thrown him in the vaults?'

'I knew you wouldn't take me seriously,' said Felicity. 'I am truly worried, Annie. Ellie doesn't need anything like this.'

Annie looked at Felicity sharply. 'Does Ellie know you think her father is missing?'

'Good Lord, no, I haven't said a thing, not to anybody apart from Mel and Martin, and Mel is already cross with me for spending so much time on Simon and not enough on baby Charlie.'

'Fair enough,' said Annie, 'I think I'd feel the same if I was her.'

'I'm serious Annie, I'm truly worried about him and this is where you come in, I was wondering whether you would pop round several times during the day and see whether there is any sign of him. You've still got your key to my place, have you?'

Annie nodded. 'Yes, of course I'll do that. I'll keep an eye out in town for him as well. I suppose he might have gone back to Oxford.'

'No,' said Felicity, 'not at the moment anyway. I've got his housekeeper on red alert. She's going to be doing the same thing as you, popping around to the house and checking whether he's there.'

'And you've tried his mobile?' Annie said.

'Yes,' said Felicity, 'I'm not completely thick.'

'Sorry, I just wondered.'

'It's going straight to answerphone.' Felicity stood up to go.

'And if he hasn't turned up by this evening?' Annie asked.

'Well, I suppose we'll have to report him as a missing person. I just don't have a good feeling about this, Annie.'

'Best get your poor long-suffering policeman involved then.'

'He's not long-suffering and he's certainly not mine,' said Felicity, firmly.

'You two have been pretty quiet back along, time you livened things up a bit. I'll ring you teatime if there's still no sign of Simon and then you'll be early enough to catch your man before he goes off duty.'

Felicity bent forward and kissed Annie warmly. 'Thanks Annie, you're a brick.'

Chief Inspector Keith Penrose sat behind his desk eyeing his sergeant, Jack Curnow, balefully. 'How did it go?' he asked.

Jack shrugged. 'Well, you know.'

'Pretty awful, was it?'

Jack nodded. 'It's odd isn't it? We had to take the little chap straight to hospital he's so badly beaten about, but he still didn't want to leave his family, put up quite a struggle.'

Keith swung his chair around, putting his back towards his sergeant, and stared down into the car park below. He hated cruelty to children. That was his nemesis – anything that hurt children, he could not bear. Social Services had asked Keith to provide back-up to remove a six-year old boy from his family. They had been served with a court order two days earlier but the family had refused to hand him over and Social Services were becoming increasingly worried that the delay would cause the child to suffer more. Keith had sent his sergeant and a couple of uniformed officers. He let out a sigh. 'So the boy's being kept overnight in hospital, is he?'

'Yes sir, a few days, two I think. He's got some broken ribs and they're worried about damage to some of his internal organs, he may lose his spleen.'

'Christ,' said Keith, turning around to face Jack, 'Six years old – I expect he's scared stiff being in hospital on his own.'

'They've appointed a foster mum, one of their more experienced women apparently. She's with him now so no, he's not alone.'

'Thank Christ for that,' said Keith, 'what a world

we live in, Jack.'

'I don't know it's changed much,' said Jack. 'We read *Oliver Twist* at school, seems we've always ill-treated our young. You don't see that happen much in the animal kingdom.'

'And we consider ourselves superior to animals,' said Keith, 'it's a joke, isn't it?'

'You seem a bit low-spirited today, sir.'

Keith was about to reply when his private line rang. He picked up the phone. 'Penrose.'

'Keith, it's Felicity here.'

'Hang on a moment.' He put a hand over the mouthpiece. 'It's Mrs Paradise.'

'Oh, OK sir,' said Jack, 'I'll leave you to it.' Jack left the office, closing the door quietly behind him. 'That'll cheer the old boy up,' he thought, with a grin.

'So he's been missing for barely thirty-six hours,' Keith said.

'It's not the length of time he's been missing,' Felicity said, patiently. 'It's the circumstances.

'OK, but I'm not sure what you want me to do?'

'I want you to find him, of course,' said Felicity.

'Certainly we can register him as a missing person but it's not like he's a child. Do you think he might be suicidal given he's just lost his wife?'

'Annie asked me that,' said Felicity. 'No, I'm sure he isn't. I'm absolutely sure in my own mind that a) he wouldn't kill himself and b) he wouldn't be so discourteous as to disappear out of my life without

126

telling me where he was going. It's just not how he'd behave. He's a very organised, correct sort of person with beautiful manners. In some respects, I have to admit, he is a bit of a bore, but he would never behave irresponsibly unless he had no choice in the matter.'

'And you say you've checked his Oxford home and you've spoken to his daughter. Have you told her he's missing?'

'No,' said Felicity, 'certainly not, not at the moment.'

'Probably wise,' said Keith. 'The trouble is, as I say, he's a grown man and he's not even a resident of Cornwall, there's not a great deal I can do.'

'Even though he could be in terrible danger?' Felicity said.

'That's your opinion,' said Keith, 'but there's no proof to back it up.'

'I've just given you the proof,' Felicity said. 'Honestly Keith, surely we've worked together long enough now that if I say there is reason to be worried, you know I'm not just being some hysterical woman.'

'I know that,' said Keith. 'Look, leave it with me and I'll see what I can do and obviously you'll let me know when he turns up.'

'Obviously,' said Felicity, 'but I think it's more a case of if, not when.'

9

Mel was in a complete state by the time Felicity returned to Hayle.

'Mum, where have you been?' she wailed. She was still in her nightdress, hair dishevelled, Charlie sobbing in her arms.

'Looking for Simon,' said Felicity.

'I thought you'd be back hours ago, Martin has gone to the Gardens and dropped Minty off at playgroup. I'm supposed to pick her up in an hour and Charlie won't stop crying and I can't find anything to wear that fits me and I didn't know when you'd be back.' Her voice ended in a crescendo as tears flooded down her cheeks.

Felicity took the crying baby from her. 'Bed,' she said firmly, 'I'll bring you a cup of tea.'

'I don't want a cup of tea,' said Mel.

'You do,' said Felicity, 'you're exhausted and your milk's coming in. Has this one been fed?'

Mel nodded, allowing herself to be led up the stairs. 'Yes, but he won't stop crying.'

'I expect he's picking up all your jangled vibes,' said Felicity. 'Now hop into bed, I'll take Charlie downstairs and make us some tea and then Charlie and I will go and collect Minty.' Charlie settled down in the crook of her arm and despite all her worries Felicity smiled to herself as she prepared Mel's tea. The art of doing everything one-handed was rather like riding a bike – it all came flooding back. While the kettle boiled, she pulled through Minty's old pram from the utility room into the kitchen and settled Charlie in it. She pushed the pram backwards and forwards a couple of times and within moments Charlie was asleep. 'You are a good baby,' said Felicity, 'so placid, not like your Grandpa.' She took two cups of tea upstairs to Mel who was almost asleep.

'Where's Charlie?' Mel said.

'Asleep in his pram, now calm down.'

'Sorry, sorry,' said Mel, pulling herself up in bed. 'I just lost the plot.'

'I know and I'm sorry,' said Felicity. 'I should have rung you only I thought Martin was waiting until I got back.'

'He was,' said Mel, 'but there was some sort of crisis at the Gardens, nothing much but …' her voice tailed away. 'I'm being hopeless, aren't I?'

'No, you're not darling – another week and you'll be fine. It's a completely different experience having a second child. With a first baby you can just focus on your newborn, with the next one you're splitting yourself in two all the time. It's hard work.'

'I forgot Simon,' said Mel, sipping her tea. 'I'm sorry, I didn't ask about him. Did you find him alright?'

Felicity shook her head. 'No, there's no sign of him.'

'I expect you just keep missing each other, he's in when you're out and vice versa.'

Felicity was about to launch into her worries concerning the untouched coffee cup and newspaper but thought better of it, Mel had enough going on. 'I expect you're right,' she said. 'Now have you any plans as to what Minty is having for lunch?'

Mel shook her head, tears welling again. 'No, I haven't, I'm hopeless.'

'Stop,' said Felicity, 'snuggle down in that bed and go to sleep. We'll pick up something from the shop on the way home, some really sophisticated culinary delight, like fish fingers.'

'Minty will do almost anything for a fish finger,' said Mel.

'I know,' said Felicity. 'Now as soon as himself gets hungry again I'll bring him up to you – until then sleep.'

It was an unusual and rather welcome role reversal, Felicity reflected, as she pulled on her coat and put a lead on Harvey ready for the walk to pick up Minty. Since Mel could first speak, she had been extremely bossy and as her father had rightly anticipated, she possessed all the makings of a serious control freak. It was rather soothing being able to tell Mel what to do for a change.

The day slipped by – feeding, changing, playing with a tired, fractious Minty who was clearly somewhat overwhelmed by the changes in routine caused by this new brother. Felicity was starting to cook supper, Martin having planted a much-needed glass of white wine by her elbow, when the phone rang.

'It's for you,' said Martin. 'Annie.'

All day, the growing concern for Simon had been hovering at the fringes of her mind but such had been the demands of family life, there had been no time to give him serious thought. Now she dropped the wooden spoon she was using to stir the casserole and ran across the room. 'Annie, any news?'

'No, my girl, not a thing. I've been in three times, in fact I'm ringing you from your cottage now, nothing has been moved, he definitely hasn't been here all day.'

'Oh Annie, what's happened to him?' Felicity asked.

'I don't know but I think it's time we started to worry. Having just lost his wife like that, it wouldn't be surprising if he'd gone doolally.'

'I'm sure it's not that, Annie. I know he was absolutely devastated by Gilla's death, always will be, but he's quite a stoical sort of chap. I just can't see him walking out on Ellie, and as for suicide, he'd never leave Ellie without a parent.'

'I think to consider suicide,' said Annie, 'you have to be in a very self-centred place. You're so wrapped up in your own problems, you don't concern yourself with how your actions will affect other people. I'll not say he has topped himself, I'm just saying that if he was in that frame of mind – and only you can judge whether he was – then Ellie would not be his major concern.'

'You're right, of course,' said Felicity with a sigh, 'you always are.'

'I reckon it's time you talked to your policeman again.'

Felicity glanced at her watch. 'It's too late now to talk to him, I'll call him first thing in the morning. Can you check the cottage for me tomorrow morning?'

'Yes, of course. I'm sorry I didn't ring earlier, I had to wait for some guests to arrive but I'm always up at five, as you know, so I'll pop over then. How early shall I call you?'

'As early as you like,' said Felicity. 'At the moment, this household operates on Charlie's hours so I'm sure I'll be up and about. Ring my mobile so as not to disturb the family in case they're asleep.'

'Will do,' said Annie.

'What's going on?' said Martin, as soon as

132

Felicity had put down the phone. 'Is Simon still missing?'

Felicity nodded, tears coming into her eyes. 'I'm so worried, Martin.'

'Have you spoken to Keith Penrose?'

Felicity nodded. 'He doesn't seem much interested. No, that's not true,' she corrected herself, 'he doesn't think there is much we can do at the moment. When I spoke to him last I didn't even know for sure that Simon was missing, just thought there was no evidence of him being around. But if he doesn't come back to the cottage tonight then he will have been away for two whole nights. That's not right, Martin.'

'And you've checked Oxford?'

'Yes, Simon and Gilla have a lovely cleaner called June. She's checking the house regularly and said she would call me if she had a sighting.'

'And Ellie?'

'Ellie hasn't heard from him either but I haven't told her that he's missing.'

'You'll have to tell her soon,' said Martin.

'I know, I was thinking that.'

'Come and sit down for a moment,' said Martin. 'You look all in. Mel's just feeding Charlie, I've turned down the casserole and I'm topping up your wine – doctor's orders.'

Felicity sat down thankfully at the kitchen table and Martin joined her.

'So I gather from what you said to Annie, you don't think he's in the frame of mind to take his own life?'

Felicity shook her head. 'No, he's just not that sort of person. I think he's been kidnapped, Martin.'

'Kidnapped?'

Felicity took him through the whole Carlyon story.

'It's far-fetched, Fizzy, isn't it?'

'Oh no, not you too,' said Felicity, 'another disbeliever. I'd have thought it was obvious – they've warned him off, threatened him but they're still worried he'll be a whistle-blower.'

'So,' said Martin, 'they kidnap him and then what, pull his toenails out until he agrees to say nothing?'

'Oh please!' said Felicity.

'Sorry, sorry but honestly, Fizzy, I think you're going off on a tangent here. Surely there are only two reasons why people get kidnapped – either for a ransom demand or because they're going to be killed.'

'And that's supposed to reassure me?' said Felicity.

'No,' said Martin, 'it's supposed to be a wake-up call. I'm not particularly fond of banks or bankers but I really don't see them going around murdering people – charging a small fortune for an unauthorised overdraft, yes – daylight robbery, but not murder.'

'Stop it, Martin, it isn't funny,' said Felicity.

'Fizzy, come on, I know tensions are running high in this house at the moment but it's not like you to lose your sense of humour. I know you're worried about Simon but he'll turn up, I'm sure of it.'

'And I'm not,' said Felicity. She scraped back her chair and stood up. 'I'm going to take Harvey for a walk and have a think.'

'Don't go off in high dudgeon, Fizzy,' said Martin standing up too.

'I'm not, I'm really not. Look, supper is ready, it will do you and Mel good to have a meal on your own without me here fussing about Simon.'

'Then we'll keep some warm for you,' said Martin.

'No don't bother, honestly, I'm not hungry.'

'Fizzy, I didn't mean to upset you.'

'I know,' said Felicity. 'I just need some space to think.'

It was a grey overcast night with a light drizzle and as soon as Felicity was out of the house, she regretted leaving. 'Sorry Harvey,' she said. She had intended to walk along the side of the estuary, maybe go down onto Porth Kidney beach but it was too dark and miserable for that. Instead she headed for the lights of the Quay House pub. It was big enough to be anonymous there and think about what she should be doing for Simon. The pub was warm and welcoming. She ordered a glass of wine and bought some pork scratchings for Harvey. Then she took herself off to a far corner and sat down.

No one was taking her seriously, which rationally she knew was understandable. A man in the early days following the unexpected loss of a much-loved wife was bound to behave unpredictably – unless they were Simon – Simon was just not the type. Something wasn't right, she knew it. As on so many times in the past, she wished her gift of second sight was something that could be conjured up when required but that had never been the case. She had never understood what triggered it but it could certainly not be relied upon now to help find Simon. She thought back to their last evening together before Martin had rung to say Mel was in labour – was it really only two days ago? She regretted the fact that they had fallen out but it had only been because she was anxious about him even then. Oh, Gilla, why did you have to leave us? At the thought of Gilla, an idea flashed into her mind. She looked around the pub; she would not be disturbing anyone by making a call.

Josh Buchanan was alone in his flat staring at the wall. Since Gilla's death, he didn't seem to have much appetite for anything, and he couldn't really understand why. He had loved her deeply, of course, but it was also the loss of what she represented which was upsetting him. Her death had bought an end to something – his youth perhaps? – and he felt so bereft.

How had Fizzy described it? They were now in the front line: yes, that was it. With Gilla's death, he was being forced to recognise his own mortality. He was supposed to be going out tonight with a girl young enough to be his daughter. He had met her at a conference at the Randolph Hotel, where she was working in reception. She was not really his type and he had cancelled their date earlier on in the evening under the pretence of pressure of work – he probably should have gone, it would have cheered him up. He toyed with the idea of ringing her back and saying he had managed to finish earlier than expected, but the thought of wining and dining, ending up in her flat or his, rather than exciting him, depressed him. God, he must be getting old. His mobile rang and he turned to it with relief, anything to escape from his own thoughts. It was Fizzy, the person he wanted to speak to more than anyone.

'Fizzy,' he said, 'how lovely to hear from you, how are things going?'

'Not well,' said Felicity. 'Simon has disappeared.' In a few succinct sentences Felicity filled him in on everything that had happened. She anticipated his reaction.

'I expect the poor man has just gone walkabout,' Josh said.

'No Josh, he hasn't gone walkabout. It's not the sort of thing he would do. He's a very predictable, very conventional man who would consider it the height of rudeness to simply disappear out of my life without telling me where he was going. Anyway, I've done enough arguing my case on this subject. I'm ringing up for a specific reason, Josh. You know the Carlyon Bank?'

'Yes, of course,' said Josh.

'Do you know anybody who works there?'

'Not who works there specifically,' said Josh, 'but I know one of the major shareholders. In fact, come to think of it, so do you.'

'You're not talking about Hugh Randall?'

'No,' said Josh, 'I don't know a Hugh Randall but I do know Adam Dakin. You must remember him, Fizzy?'

Fizzy thought hard. 'I don't think I do.'

'He was a friend of Charlie's, in fact they were at Eton together, tremendously overweight, rather bombastic over-confident sort of chap. Lives alone in a wonderfully elegant house just off Sloane Square, since his wife left him.'

'Has an opinion on everything, goes purple in the face if he doesn't get his own way?'

'Exactly,' said Josh, 'you do remember him?'

'I do,' said Felicity, 'he was one of the people I could never understand why Charlie liked so much. We had him to dinner periodically and he never failed to mention that it was quaint having supper in the kitchen. He was obviously used to chandeliers, mahogany tables, best silver and a butler.'

'I imagine that's how he dines every night,' said Josh. 'Anyway, I'm glad you remember him. He is my only contact with Carlyon's as far as I know.'

'Do you think you could fix up for me to go and see him urgently?'

'I would imagine so,' said Josh, 'but what on earth are you going to say to him, Fizzy?'

'I'm going to ask if he's kidnapped Simon, of course.'

Josh rang her back shortly after ten the following morning.

'I've got you an appointment with Adam,' he said, 'it's for eleven o'clock tomorrow morning, can you make it?'

'Yes,' said Felicity, with more confidence than she felt.

'He has an office just off the Strand by the Law Courts.' Josh gave her the address. 'How will you get there?' he asked.

'Train,' said Felicity. 'The first train out of Penzance in the morning gets into Paddington at ten o'clock, I should just make it.'

'That's perfect,' said Josh. 'I'll just telephone his secretary and confirm the appointment.'

'Thanks Josh. Did he ask what it was about?'

'Yes,' said Josh.

'And what did you say?'

'I said I hadn't the least idea but it would be a

nice gesture to see you for Charlie's sake. He agreed.'

'Good,' said Felicity, 'I didn't want him to have any warning of what I was going to talk about.'

'Honestly Fizzy, he's going to think you're round the bend. I really can't see old Adam involved in a kidnap plot.'

'I'm desperate Josh,' said Fizzy, simply. 'I'm not suggesting Adam is involved but making a fuss at shareholder level should cause a reaction of some sort.'

To organise plans for the next twenty-four hours needed a great deal of tact and diplomacy. Mel's emotions were still all over the place. As soon as Felicity mentioned that she would be away for a day, Mel threw a tantrum.

'Honestly Mother, you care more about Simon that you do about your own grandson.'

'You know that's rubbish, Mel,' said Felicity, 'but I do have a very real sense of responsibility towards Ellie. She's already lost one parent and now the other one is missing. She is my goddaughter, I've got to do something.'

'And I'm your daughter,' Mel wailed. 'Can't wonder boy Penrose sort it out? You're going on a complete wild goose chase.'

'Very probably,' said Felicity, 'but I have to try and no, there doesn't seem to be much the police can do at present.'

She decided that such was Mel's fragile state, having a dog to look after would be the final straw, so she arranged for Annie to take Harvey.

'I'll drop him over tonight, if that's OK, because I've got a very early start in the morning but I should be back in St Ives early evening.'

'That's alright, you take your time. You know I'm fond of that little dog, we'll have a lovely day.'

The other part of her plan was particularly sensitive.

'Ellie, it's Fizzy here. How are things going?'

'Not too bad,' Ellie replied. 'I'm still finding it hard to concentrate though, but at least I've no lectures this week.'

'Perfect,' said Felicity. 'I've got to go up to London tomorrow, unexpectedly. I was thinking – why don't you come down to Cornwall, sooner rather than later? Make a long weekend of it; it's such a long way to come from Edinburgh for just a day or two.'

'I'm not sure,' said Ellie. 'I have a pile of work to do,'

'You can bring it with you.'

'Does Dad want me to come?'

'I'm sure he does,' Felicity said, carefully.

'Why are you coming up to London?' Ellie asked.

'Oh, I just need to see a publisher about some illustrations,' Felicity lied. 'My meeting will be over by midday. Could you get an early train into King's Cross and then we could travel down to Cornwall together? My car will be at Penzance station. It's lovely down here, at the moment, really warm. Come on Ellie, it'll do you good.'

'It certainly seems to be suiting Dad, I never hear from him.' There was a poignant pause, during which Felicity held her breath.

'OK, OK, I'll text you my train times as soon as I've organised the journey.'

'Brilliant, have you got enough money?' Felicity asked.

'Yes, I'm fine.'

'OK, see you tomorrow then.' Felicity put the phone down with a huge sigh of relief. She hated telling lies to Ellie but there was no way she could tell her over the phone that her father was missing. God knew how she was going to tell her anyway.

10

Chief Inspector Keith Penrose and his sergeant, Jack Curnow, were sitting glumly in Keith's office surrounded, as always, by his paperwork. Things were particularly quiet in West Cornwall. Even the previous Saturday night celebrations across the county had been more subdued than usual, a result presumably of the credit crunch. It left both men unusually underemployed.

'I think we should try to find this Simon Carter,' said Keith, knocking back his cup of coffee and grimacing at the disgusting nature of its contents.

'He's just gone AWOL sir, hasn't he? He's lost his wife – grief affects people in lots of different ways. I suppose he might top himself.'

'Mrs Paradise says not,'

'Well, she would know,' said Jack, with a smile.

'I agree,' said Keith, Jack's irony completely lost on him. 'I think we owe her this one, Jack, she has been very helpful to us in the past. This man is the father of her goddaughter, the husband of her best

143

friend. We couldn't take it on if we had something more pressing to do, but we don't.'

'So what do you think has happened to him then, sir?'

Keith shrugged. 'Mrs Paradise thinks he has been kidnapped by a bunch of bankers.'

Jack gave a short laugh. 'Well she would, wouldn't she?'

'You may mock, Jack,' said Keith, 'but she's usually right, isn't she?'

'Yes,' Jack admitted, 'but surely this one is going a bit far – kidnapped by bankers!'

Keith chose to ignore him. 'If you're going to kidnap someone and hold them somewhere in West Cornwall, what would you do?'

'But why hold him here, sir? Surely if they are bankers from up country they would take him back up there with them, take him to a place they know.'

'We're talking West Cornwall, Jack, because that's our patch.'

'So we're getting the crime to fit the investigation, rather than the investigation fit the crime?'

'Something like that,' Keith said, allowing himself a smile. 'Just humour me, would you?'

Jack frowned in concentration. 'Well it's the end of the season isn't it, shouldn't be too difficult to rent a cottage at relatively short notice.'

'My sentiments exactly,' said Keith, 'there are

plenty of cottages off the beaten track where you could hold someone without any fear of detection.'

'So you want me to...?' Jack began.

'Get hold of the agents, particularly in the St Ives area and see if anyone has made a recent late booking at a particularly remote cottage – a man, that should close the gap a little.'

'Why a man?' said Jack. 'That's a bit sexist isn't it, sir?'

'Simon Carter is a big bloke,' said Keith, patiently. 'About six foot two, broad with it. I don't see a woman being able to restrain him against his will, not unless she was some sort of Amazon.'

'Before I start all this, sir, you're sure he hasn't turned up?'

'Mrs Paradise would have let me know if he had, but just to satisfy you, I was going to make contact with her anyway because we need an up-to-date photograph.'

'OK sir, so I'll get cracking shall I?'

'Yes,' said Keith, 'and I'll alert the Missing Persons Unit and see what they will do to help us.'

'I can't help thinking this is all a bit of a wild goose chase sir, if I may say so.'

'No, you may not,' said Keith, 'now hop it.'

'Where are you?' Keith said. 'You sound like you're at the bottom of a tin can?'

'I'm at the station,' said Felicity, 'booking a ticket

for tomorrow for London.'

'Why are you going to London, if I may ask?' Keith said.

'I'm going to beard Carlyon Bank in their lair; well, in particular one of their shareholders.'

'To achieve what?' Keith was amazed.

'Well to find out if they've kidnapped Simon, of course.'

'Oh, so you think they're going to tell you, do you?' Keith said, smiling at the thought of Felicity barging into the boardroom of a city bank and demanding they hand over her friend.

'I've got to do something,' Felicity said, 'you're not doing anything.'

'As a matter of fact I am,' said Keith. 'I'm getting Jack to investigate the possibility that Simon might be being held against his will in a rented cottage somewhere in the area and I'm asking the Missing Persons Unit to help us find him. They normally achieve very good results.'

'Thank you,' said Felicity, humbly.

'The reason I was ringing is to ask if you have got an recent photograph of Simon?'

'No,' said Felicity, 'of course there are plenty at their Oxfordshire home but I'm not going anywhere near Oxford. I need to come back to Cornwall tomorrow night as I'm bringing his daughter, Ellie, back with me.'

'How's she taking the news?'

'I don't know yet,' said Felicity, 'I haven't told her. I didn't want to tell her while she was all alone at university. I'm picking her up off the train while I'm in London and we'll travel down together. That'll be time enough to tell her that her father is missing – or maybe you'll have found him by then.' There was a silence. 'Keith, are you still there?' Felicity asked.

'Yes,' said Keith. 'I was just thinking of Ellie.'

'And?' Felicity asked.

'I was just relating it to Carly, imagining what it must be like to lose your mother so unexpectedly and then have your father go missing.'

'It's awful,' said Felicity. 'I don't know how to tell her, but at least you have your incentive now, Chief Inspector. Hold that image of how Carly would feel in similar circumstances.'

'I will. Now you won't behave too outrageously at the Bank, will you? You can't start throwing accusations around without any foundation for them.'

'I will be the soul of tact,' said Felicity.

'Well, that will be a first,' said Keith. 'What about a photograph?'

'When I was looking in his room yesterday I saw his passport, which at least shows he hasn't skipped the country. I didn't look at the photograph, I just noticed that he hadn't taken his passport with him. If my passport photograph is anything to go by he'll look like a mad axeman, but I can certainly let you have it. There's no reason why I shouldn't catch the early train from Truro instead of Penzance in the morning, I'll drop it into the station on my way.'

'Will that be alright?' said Keith. 'It'll be some hideous hour of the morning.'

'That's fine, and Keith, you will do your best, won't you? This is serious now, he's been missing too long. I'm not being paranoid or overdramatic or any of the other things that I so frequently get accused of – Simon is missing and something bad has happened.'

'I really will do my best,' said Keith, 'I'm sorry if I was rather flippant before, it's just that we get this sort of thing all the time – some sort of domestic which ends up with somebody disappearing for a few days to cool off. We'll pull out all the stops now and see what we can find.'

'Thanks,' said Felicity. 'I'll ring you when I'm back from London.'

'No blood on the carpet, no hurling paper weights about?'

'The soul of decorum,' Felicity promised.

11

The day so far had run like clockwork but the smooth running of her schedule had done nothing to allay Felicity's nerves. She had left St Ives at 4.30 a.m. Driving out of the silent town, the morning was pitch dark, Winter was just round the corner. She had dropped off Simon's passport with the duty officer at Truro police station, driven to the station, parked her car and caught the 5.46 for Paddington with plenty of time to spare. Amazingly, the train had rolled into Paddington at ten o'clock sharp, she had given Adam Dakin's address to a taxi driver and now she was sitting in a coffee shop five minutes' walk away from his office with half an hour to kill – plenty of time for her nerves to get the better of her.

The proposed meeting with Adam Dakin now seemed ridiculous. Keith had been right, marching into his office and accusing him of kidnapping Simon Carter was not really an option, yet that was essentially why she was here. She would have to play it by ear. All she could remember about Dakin was that he presented as a pompous, overweight old buffer with charming manners but an over-developed sense of his own importance. That was probably the way she should handle him, pander to his own sense of self worth. She stared down into her cooling cup of coffee. She felt decidedly queasy but not because of the forthcoming meeting with Adam Dakin; it was what was to follow that was upsetting her. She was due to meet Ellie at King's Cross shortly after one o'clock and Felicity just could not begin to work out how to handle things. There was the sheer logistics to consider – in order to be in time for the Paddington train back to Truro, they would have to take a taxi from King's Cross to Paddington. Should she tell Ellie in the taxi that her father was missing; should she wait until they were on the train with perhaps an entire carriage listening in; should she wait until they were in the privacy of her car driving back to St Ives? No, that was impossible, she couldn't possibly keep the news from Ellie for that long, she would have to tell her right away in the taxi. She couldn't bear to think how Ellie would feel, the whole situation was a nightmare. Her stomach was in knots, her head ached; she was certainly not in the right frame of mind to be dynamic with Adam Dakin. She glanced at her watch. Ten minutes to go. She might as well wander across the road; there was no harm in being a few minutes early.

* * *

Keith looked up from his desk as Jack came into his office.

'Any luck?' Keith asked.

'Results up to a point, sir,' said Jack

'Go on,' said Keith.

'Across all the agents dealing with cottages and flats in West Cornwall there have been twenty-three late bookings.'

'Twenty-three, blast,' said Keith.

'No, wait sir, it's not that bad. We've been able to eliminate fifteen of those straight away because they're repeat bookings from regular clients.'

'So that leaves eight,' said Keith.

'Yes.'

'And how many of those were made by men?'

'That's the trouble really sir, most bookings these days are made on the internet and it's not always easy to tell. I do have one telephone booking made by a male, a Tom Darcy. The area is right – a fairly isolated cottage just outside St Erth. He made the booking in person to a St Ives agency and paid in cash.'

'Now that does sound hopeful,' said Keith.

'Yes, I'm on my way to check it out now, and the others if I have no luck with this first one. I thought I'd make a day of it, sir, unless you need me for anything else?'

'No, good idea,' said Keith, 'but take someone with you just in case there is any trouble.'

'Do you really think it is likely?'

Keith shrugged. 'I don't know, I've got no feel at all for this one, Jack, it all seems so implausible, somehow.'

'So are we turning it into a full-scale inquiry?' Jack asked.

'I don't imagine the Super will think too much of it, a waste of police resources and all that, but Missing Persons think it's worth a punt and suggested I put out an appeal on Spotlight tomorrow.'

'Why not today?' Jack said.

'I'm not exactly sure when Mrs Paradise is telling Simon Carter's daughter about his disappearance. I know she is bringing the girl down to Cornwall today but I don't want to run the risk of her turning on the television and finding an appeal for her missing father before Mrs Paradise has had a chance to break the news to her. Besides, another twelve hours still gives him a chance to turn up. Let me know when you've made any progress.'

'Will do,' said Jack.

Adam Dakin was even larger than Felicity remembered. He rose from behind his enormous desk like a huge whale erupting out of the ocean. He waddled round to greet her with some difficulty, enveloping her in a huge embrace in which she thought she might suffocate.

'Felicity, my dear, how wonderful to see you, quite made my day, you look enchanting! Come and

152

sit down, coffee, tea, juice, something stronger?'

A secretary hovered nearby, awaiting instructions.

'Nothing, thank you,' said Felicity. 'I was a little early for my appointment so I've just had a cup of coffee across the way.'

'You should have come straight in to see me, not loitered in some unsavoury coffee house.'

'Well, I know you're a busy man,' Felicity began, remembering the need to pander to his ego.

'I am, I am, but never too busy to see you. I'm so sorry about Charlie, I wrote to you at the time of course, but you've been on my conscience. How are you coping with your loss?'

'It's been six years now,' said Felicity, 'I've had time to adjust.'

'Six years, is it really, good heavens!' Having collapsed back in his chair, Adam produced a handkerchief and mopped his brow.

This man has serious problems, Felicity thought. He can't be long for this world if walking round his desk brings him out in a sweat. His complexion had a dangerous, mottled look and his breathing, she realised, was a little wheezy. He's committing suicide by inches.

'When Josh Buchanan telephoned to say you'd like to see me I suggested that maybe you'd join me for lunch. I hope he passed the message on and that you're free.'

The thought of watching this man stuff himself with yet more food and drink was so deplorable that Felicity had to resist the urge to shudder. 'That's very kind of you Adam, but I'm afraid I can't. I'm picking someone up from King's Cross around one o'clock.'

'That is a shame,' Adam wheezed. 'There is a wonderful new Italian just opened, it's less than three minutes in a taxi from here. We could have an early lunch, I suppose?'

It would do you more good to walk to your new Italian, Felicity thought, than to spend three minutes in a taxi. She smiled at him, hoping the insincerity didn't show. 'Bless you, Adam. No, the schedule is too tight and in any case I've only just had breakfast on the train.'

He looked crestfallen and then made a visible effort to perk up. 'Your children, they must be quite grown up now. Did I hear a rumour that your girl has followed her father into law?'

'Yes,' said Felicity.

'Wasn't she articled to Michael Ferguson? He's a QC now, quite the rising star; your girl did well to join forces with him.'

'She no longer works for him,' said Felicity. 'She's married with children now and has joined a firm in Truro.'

'Truro!' exclaimed Adam, making it sound like Outer Mongolia. 'What on earth made her pick on Truro?'

'Her husband is Cornish and I live down there, too.'

'So you have forsaken Oxford? What an strange thing to do, Felicity.'

'Not at all. I live in St Ives and I absolutely love it.'

'Extraordinary,' said Adam. He was silent for a moment, clearly digesting the concept that anyone should choose to live so far from civilization, as he saw it. He recovered his composure. 'So tell me, what can I do for you?'

Felicity took a deep breath gazing around her. The walls of Adam's enormous office were papered with portraits of presumably long-gone Dakins – they were certainly a well-fed bunch. She had purposely not rehearsed what she was going to say, the only thing to do was just go for it. 'I understand, Adam, that you are a shareholder in the Carlyon Bank.'

Adam looked taken aback. 'Yes I am. Do you bank with us?'

'No, no I don't,' said Felicity.

'You want to invest?' Adam began.

'No, no this isn't about money Adam, can I just explain?'

'Yes, of course.' He made a great play of sitting back on his chair and assuming an enquiring expression.

'Have you ever heard of a man called Simon Carter?'

Adam thought for a moment and shook his head. 'No, should I?'

'He worked for Carlyon for some years, in your Hong Kong branch.' She watched him closely but could see no sense of discomfort.

'Right,' said Adam. 'The name doesn't mean anything to me, I have to confess, but then of course we have thousands of employees.'

'Quite so,' said Felicity. 'Simon left the bank under something of a cloud three years ago.'

'I'm sorry to hear that. Is he a friend of yours?'

'Yes,' said Felicity.

'And what was his misdemeanour?'

'None, anyway none that I can understand,' Felicity replied. 'He reported direct to your Chairman, Hugh Randall. He believed there to be trouble brewing in the Hong Kong branch. Apparently, there had been a great many unwise investments made. This is a field I know absolutely nothing about, Adam, but I understand that the Bank had committed to some fairly wild investments which were unsupported by appropriate security. Simon was Financial Controller for the Far East and he reported his findings to Hugh Randall.'

'So what happened?' Adam asked.

'Hugh Randall sacked him.'

'I find that very hard to believe, my dear,' said Adam. His expression had changed. Formerly it had been patronising, now it was alert.

'I can assure you that is what happened.'

'So what do you want me to do about it? It is rather a long time ago, are you suggesting there is a case for unfair dismissal or something?'

'No,' said Felicity. 'As it happens Simon was happy to leave the Bank. He had made his report to your Chairman, he felt he was vindicated by doing so and that was that so far as his relationship with Carlyon was concerned.'

'So?' Adam said, raising an eyebrow.

'Adam, tragically Simon's wife died a few weeks ago. Hugh Randall attended the funeral and afterwards invited Simon out to lunch. During that lunch he threatened Simon.'

'Threatened him, that doesn't sound like Hugh's style. What do you mean, threatened him?' Adam was becoming agitated, his breathing erratic.

'Well, perhaps threatened is going too far,' Felicity admitted, 'but he wanted Simon's assurance that he would not disclose to anyone the contents of his report concerning the irregularities in Hong Kong. As I understand it Carlyon is in trouble and is hoping for a Government bail-out. An inappropriate word to the press at this moment could presumably rock the boat.'

Adam stared at Felicity with surprising shrewdness. He was silent for a moment. 'So what are you here to do, blackmail me?'

'Oh for heaven's sake!' Felicity stood up and

started marching about the room. 'Adam, I am Charlie Paradise's wife, we've known each other for years, do you seriously imagine that I am the sort of person who would come here and blackmail you?'

'In my experience, money, or the lack of it, makes people do strange things,' Adam said, 'but certainly, my dear, for Charlie's sake, if you are in trouble financially I'd be only too happy to make you an unsecured loan on a low level of interest. It's the least I can …'

'Shut up, Adam,' Felicity broke in, all hope of diplomacy gone. 'I don't need your money, that's not why I'm here.'

'Then would you please tell me why you *are* here?' Adam said, his anger rising to meet hers.

This is not going well, Felicity thought. She returned to her seat with as much dignity as she could muster.

'Simon Carter has gone missing,' she said. 'I'm worried that it is because he represents a threat to the Bank.'

'My dear girl, what a ludicrous suggestion.'

'Is it?' said Felicity. 'Have you heard of a man called Alex Button?' Just for an instant, between the folds of flesh, Felicity saw the sign she had been looking for – alarm and recognition in Adam Dakin's eyes.

'Never heard of him any more than I've heard of Simon Carter,' he replied a little too hurriedly.

'Alex Button was shot a couple of days ago in Hong Kong – a city where I understand there is virtually no crime.'

'And this should mean something to me?' Adam asked.

'It certainly should,' said Felicity. 'Alex Button worked for your bank for many years and it was Alex's inappropriate investments which caused Simon Carter the most concern. Apparently, the Bank sacked him about a week ago and twenty-four hours later he was found with a bullet in his head and apparently high on drink and drugs.'

'Well, obviously he couldn't take being sacked, which is most unfortunate,' replied Adam, now avoiding eye contact altogether.

'He didn't do drink or drugs and he didn't pull the trigger of the gun that shot him,' Felicity continued relentlessly

'I'm sorry, I'm not quite following this,' Adam said.

Felicity took a deep breath. 'I'm very concerned about the way Carlyon is treating people who they feel represent a threat to them. Alex Button is dead and Simon Carter is missing. Simon Carter is a very close friend of mine. He disappeared from my cottage in St Ives, his daughter is my goddaughter, and it is she I'm about to meet at King's Cross. I'm going to have to tell her that her father is missing, having lost her mother only weeks ago.'

Adam Dakin did not miss a beat. 'I'm really sorry about your goddaughter and of course for you too, but if the man has just lost his wife, surely the most likely explanation for his disappearance is that he is in a severe state of grief. He's either taken himself off to be alone with his grief or God forbid, he's taken his own life, because he can't cope with the loss of his wife. I really can't see what on earth this has got to do with Carlyon?'

'So are you saying,' said Felicity, 'you know nothing about your Bank's problems in Hong Kong and nothing about either Alex Button or Simon Carter?'

'Our bank, like every other bank in the Western world at the moment, is struggling. I'm sure even in,' he frowned, 'even in St Ives, you will have been aware that there is a worldwide financial crisis unfolding but I don't think that means…' he paused and allowed himself a smile, 'that the Bank has started shooting its staff.' He gave a stupid little laugh, 'not yet anyway.'

'So you're not going to help me?'

'I can't.'

'Will you talk to Hugh Randall for me?'

'Next time I see him I'll certainly mention your concerns. If, as you say, he knows this Simon Carter personally he will obviously be very sad to hear of his disappearance. I shouldn't worry.' Adam leant forward across the desk. 'I'm sure he'll turn up soon.'

* * *

'Complete bloody waste of time,' Felicity muttered to herself as she climbed into another taxi en route to King's Cross. 'I'm not even going to think of how many days' work I'll need to do to pay for all these taxis.' She leant back in the seat and gazed out of the window at London as it flew by. She re-ran the meeting in her mind, Adam had appeared totally relaxed and avuncular throughout except for that one moment when she had first mentioned Alex Button's name. He had known precisely who Alex was and presumably what had happened to him. Therefore if he had lied about Alex he could lie about Simon.

An awful thought struck her. Had she made Simon's position more dangerous by this confrontational meeting? Had she put her own life in danger? She imagined Adam ringing his secretary and ordering a giant cheeseburger and a hit man to take out Felicity Paradise; it didn't seem terribly likely but everything surrounding Simon's disappearance seemed unreal. Anyway the deed was done now. Hugh Randall would soon know that Simon had told someone else about his report and if he had confided in Felicity, who else might he have told? There was satisfaction in imagining his discomfiture, if nothing else.

She glanced out of the window. They were on the Marylebone Road now, not long to go. Her heart lurched. She pulled out her mobile phone from her bag and dialled Annie's number in the forlorn hope that Simon might have turned up and the grisly task ahead of her might not be necessary.

12

Chief Inspector Keith Penrose had spent a busy, but apparently fruitless day. Jack Curnow had drawn a blank. All the last-minute holiday bookings had proved legitimate, including the St Erth cottage. Following a particularly nasty bout of flu which had afflicted his wife and three small children, Tom Darcy had made the snap decision to bring them all down to Cornwall for a week's sea air. At the suggestion of the Missing Persons Unit, Keith had organised house to house enquiries at all the cottages either side and opposite Jericho Cottage hoping that someone might have witnessed Simon's abduction, if such a thing had happened. Being St Ives, everyone already knew that Simon was staying with Felicity Paradise and of the loss of his wife but no one had seen anything even vaguely suspicious, just him coming and going. There were absolutely no leads. Keith presumed that Simon had disappeared sometime between late on Monday night and three o'clock on Tuesday afternoon. After cooking him supper on Monday, Felicity had received the call from Martin Tregonning saying his wife was in labour and she had left Simon at about ten o'clock. She seemed convinced that by the time she returned the following afternoon with Minty to collect some clothes, Simon had already vanished. He would have to ask her why that was. Keith glanced at his watch. It was just after one o'clock – either she was rattling the cage of Carlyon Bank or collecting Simon Carter's poor daughter from the train – either way he felt he could not disturb her.

After a hurried sandwich, Keith returned to his desk. Simon's passport photo had been circulated to all the local media and sent to Thames Valley Police so that a similar campaign could be launched in Oxford. At 2.30 Keith gave an interview to BBC Spotlight with an embargo on it until the following day for Ellie's protection. There seemed very little more he could do. He was conscious that it was now Thursday and that a full day had been wasted while he had waited for Simon to turn up of his own volition. He felt bad about that, while at the same time knowing feelings of guilt were inappropriate since he was making far more fuss about the disappearance of Simon Carter than would normally be applied so soon to an adult missing person. Two things had influenced his decision to launch a full scale search. Firstly, he knew Felicity Paradise's instincts could be trusted and secondly, he just wanted to do something to help her.

* * *

164

Ellie sat frozenly in the back of the taxi, staring straight ahead of her. She had allowed Felicity to take one of her hands and hold it, but as always she remained composed, letting none of her feelings show. She was so very different from her mother, Felicity thought with a pang. Gilla had always said whatever had come into her head and if that had involved screaming or crying, it wouldn't matter where they were, out it would all pour. Ellie had lost weight in the last few weeks and it suited her. She had gone very pale but seemed completely in control.

'So he didn't give you any clue that he was planning to go anywhere?'

'No,' said Felicity.

'And did he appear particularly upset?'

'No,' Felicity said, 'and in case you're thinking he might have committed suicide, honestly Ellie, I don't think that's an option.'

'I agree,' said Ellie, turning to face her godmother and surprising Felicity with the sureness of her response. 'Dad's just not the sort of person to do anything so extreme.' She allowed herself the ghost of a smile. 'Now Mum, of course, would have been a completely different matter. I can see her in a drunken rage of grief throwing herself off a cliff, lots of drama and wild red hair.' As she spoke Ellie's lip trembled and tears appeared in the green eyes that were so like Gilla's. 'I miss her so much,' she whispered to Felicity.

Felicity squeezed her hand. 'Me too,' she said.

'So what do you think has happened to him?' Ellie asked.

The taxi turned into Spring Street. Felicity glanced at her watch. 'We've got a good forty minutes before our train leaves and I've already bought our tickets. Let's go up to the bar and have a stiff drink and I'll tell you all about the Carlyon Bank.'

Ellie frowned. 'Carlyon Bank, who Dad used to work for?'

Felicity nodded.

'You think they're involved in his disappearance?'

The taxi swooped down into Paddington Station. 'Let's wait until we've got our drinks and I'll tell you my theory, but it is just that, Ellie, just a theory. The honest truth, darling, is that I just don't know what has happened to your father.'

Adam Dakin decided to delay his call until everyone had left the office. He often worked late. His wife had left him years ago for a younger slimmer model. He lived alone in a beautiful but soulless house in Chelsea which he used purely to sleep in. He never entertained there and he never ate there, apart from an occasional breakfast – in fact since Alice left, his life had revolved entirely around work, even his social life was now entirely work-related. He would confront Hugh Randall and having done so would reward himself with a meal at the Italian restaurant to which

166

he had intended to take Felicity Paradise.

Adam frowned; he had never quite understood what old Charlie had seen in her. She was a nice-looking woman and had worn very well, he had to admit, but she was not their type, his or Charlie's. She was too – he struggled for the word – *bohemian*, that was it. She always wore those wild colours and had some odd friends. He seemed to recall some extraordinary meals in the Paradise kitchen. In amongst children's homework and Charlie's legal briefs. Absolute chaos – he shuddered at the memory. Still, she had seemed to make old Charlie happy and there had been two nice little children. It was a damn shame she had been widowed so young but she would find someone else, bound to with her looks, unlike himself. He was doomed to monogamous living because of his sheer size; no woman would ever look at him as he was. Shaking himself out of his sense of self-pity, he lumbered to his feet, crossed his office, opened his door and peered out. As he suspected his secretary had gone. He walked back to his desk. His breathing had become very bad of late. He sat down heavily in his chair and reaching into his left-hand drawer, he found his nebuliser and took several deep puffs; that was better. Then he reached into his bottom drawer and pulled out a bottle of malt whisky and a glass – a quick snifter, he thought, before he tackled Hugh.

* * *

167

As Adam Dakin was pouring his generous measure of malt, Felicity and Ellie were sitting side by side at Exeter waiting for the train to pull out of the station for its continuing journey west. They had spoken little on the journey so far. Felicity, much to her shame, had fallen asleep somewhere near Reading and had apologised profusely, it seemed so callous. Ellie had dismissed her apologies and had seemed disinclined to talk. Now they had most of the carriage to themselves as there had been a mass exodus at Exeter. The train suddenly lurched forward and they were off again.

'I've been thinking,' said Ellie. 'I believe you could be right about Dad, being kidnapped, however far-fetched it sounds. I just cannot imagine any other explanation. I'm absolutely certain he wouldn't kill himself however sad he is about Mum and I just can't see him disappearing out of our lives without telling you or me where he was going. He wouldn't be that unkind, would he?'

Felicity shook her head. 'No, I don't believe he would. I know he's not the world's best communicator but he's been very worried about you and he is a very responsible person, I just know he wouldn't abandon you.'

'What about an accident?' said Ellie, in a small voice.

'It's possible,' said Felicity, 'but even at this time of year St Ives is still fairly densely populated. Even if

168

he was up on the cliff path there would be people up there too. If he fell and hurt himself someone would have spotted him.'

'What about swimming out too far?' Ellie said, her voice tremulous.

'Again, a swimmer in trouble anywhere in St Ives Bay is bound to be spotted.'

'But what if he had gone swimming at night or first thing in the morning when there weren't many people around?'

'Possible,' said Felicity, 'but unlikely. At this time of year it's just too cold for late night swims and he is not a particularly early riser. I'm so sorry I had to leave him alone, Ellie.'

'You couldn't do anything else. Of course you had to go and look after Minty. I'm very conscious that you should probably be helping Mel now, shouldn't you, rather than dashing up to London to try and help me and Dad?'

'Mel is OK,' said Felicity, 'she has a wonderfully supportive husband.' The image of Mel's furious face when she had told her she would be away for two nights and a day swam into Felicity's mind. She dismissed it hurriedly.

'Do you think the police will have found out anything while you've been away?' Ellie asked.

'If anything significant had happened I know they would have telephoned me,' she smiled at Ellie, encouragingly. 'So, no news is good news in a way.'

'I suppose,' said Ellie.

'Hugh, it's Adam Dakin.'

'Adam, how are you? I am hoping to have some good news for you tomorrow, things are progressing very well.'

'Meaning?' Adam asked.

'The Chancellor has agreed all the terms; the lawyers are thrashing out the final details now. I think we will be able to make the announcement tomorrow.'

'Carlyon saved but no longer ours,' Adam said.

'Still ours,' said Hugh, 'with just an extra shareholder in the form of the taxpayer.' He gave a short bark of a laugh. 'Who is likely to be the least troublesome member of the board, I suspect.'

'I imagine we're going to be very closely monitored?'

'I doubt it,' said Hugh. 'No one is suggesting the bail-out is necessary because of any fault of ours, it's the global economy that has caused our current embarrassment. The Government aren't in the banking business, nor do they want to be.'

'So they know nothing of the wild investments we've been making out in Hong Kong in the last few years?' Adam said.

There was a slight pause. 'What do you mean, Adam?' Hugh asked.

'I had a disturbing meeting today,' said Adam. 'A

woman came to see me, her name is Felicity Paradise, does that mean anything to you?'

'Nothing at all,' said Hugh.

'She is concerned about her missing friend. His name is Simon Carter, have you perhaps heard of him?'

'Of course I've heard of Simon Carter,' said Hugh Randall. 'He used to work for us. He was Financial Controller of the Far East and based in Hong Kong until a few years ago. He had been estranged from his wife but when he was over visiting me to report on Hong Kong, he took up with her again and decided to stay over here. We parted company amicably, I think.'

'I think you've applied some spin to that story,' said Adam. 'As I understand it, he came to see you because he was deeply concerned about the investments being made in Hong Kong. For whatever reason, you chose to ignore him. All this happened three years ago so God knows what the true state of our portfolio is now. Toxic assets are the words which spring to mind.'

'Adam, everything is fine, I've just told you. The Government are entirely satisfied with the Bank's performance. We're in the clear, we've managed to fight our way out of the mess.'

'There shouldn't be a mess,' said Adam, 'and you shouldn't still be Chairman of the Bank.'

'Adam, I know what I'm doing,' Hugh Randall thundered down the phone.

'And what about Alex Button?'

'What about him?'

'He's dead, I understand. Shot in Hong Kong to silence him I presume, Hugh. You've certainly made a good job of that.'

'I don't know where you're getting your information,' said Hugh, 'but you're entirely wrong.'

'I don't think so,' said Adam, 'and I don't like any of it. We had trouble with Alex Button before, as I recall, which was why you moved him to Hong Kong. Why wasn't he properly supervised, how come he got up to his old tricks again and why is he dead, Hugh, why is he dead?' In his agitation Adam could feel his breathing becoming laboured again and there was a tightness across his chest. He took a quick gulp of malt; the liquid scorched down his throat, easing his breathing for a moment.

'I fired Alex Button for incompetence,' Hugh Randall was saying, 'but I gave him a very generous package and I expect he's been spending it all on Hong Kong's low life. The Hong Kong police told me that he was so full of drink and drugs that if the bullet hadn't killed him, he would probably have died anyway. I don't know what you're insinuating, Adam?'

'A man gets shot, a man goes missing hours before we are due to receive a Government bail-out. It doesn't look good, Hugh. I'm starting to subscribe to Felicity Paradise's theory that the Carlyon Bank will stop at nothing to see this deal through. Well, not in my name, Hugh, not in mine.'

'This Felicity Paradise,' Hugh said, ignoring Adam's protests, 'how does she fit into all this?'

'As I said, she is a friend of Simon Carter. I believe she was particularly close to his wife who died recently.'

'Yes, I know about that,' said Hugh, 'I was at the funeral.' There was a slight pause. 'Would she have been the woman supporting Simon and his daughter – small, fair, forties?'

'That's the one,' said Adam, reluctantly. Instinctively, he did not like the idea of Felicity being known to Hugh Randall.

'And Simon went to stay with her in Cornwall somewhere?'

'You seem to know a lot about this,' said Adam.

'Only because it's what Simon told me. I had lunch with him to commiserate after his wife died. And you're saying he's disappeared?'

'Yes,' said Adam.

'Well I'd have thought it was fairly obvious, isn't it. The poor chap was deeply upset by the loss of his wife. He's probably topped himself or just decided he needs time alone.'

'Felicity Paradise doesn't think so,' Adam said.

'Felicity Paradise needs to mind her own business. She sounds something of a loose cannon, I don't want her sounding off her daft theories to anyone so close to the deal. Where is she now, Adam, and who is she likely to talk to? We can't have her messing things up at this late stage.'

Fear gripped Adam, not for himself but for Felicity. 'I don't know where she is, Hugh, but I'm absolutely certain she is not going to talk to anybody. She said her piece to me because I am an old friend of her late husband. She was meeting up with Simon Carter's daughter who will undoubtedly be absorbing all her time in the next twenty-four hours. The girl must be absolutely distraught having lost two parents in as many weeks. There is no need to worry about Felicity Paradise, she's ...' he struggled for breath. 'She's not a threat to you. It's not Felicity you should be worrying about, it's me.'

'And what do you mean by that, Adam?' said Hugh, his voice heavy with menace.

'I don't know I can condone this deal. I detest the idea of the Government pledging taxpayers' money to shore up a bank which has clearly been so badly managed that it is vastly over-extended. I also cannot support the concept that there should be no plans to change the management structure, and in particular, the Bank's Chairman.'

'I'm not God, Adam, you can hardly hold me responsible for the global economy. Just think about the implications of disturbing this deal. Not only would you lose all your money but if the Bank collapsed there would be hundreds and thousands of small investors who would lose theirs too. The Bank's collapse would create panic throughout the whole financial world. The Government would be forced to shore up every ailing bank, the UK economy might well be brought to its knees – we'd be a third world country before you know it. Just get a grip, Adam … Adam?'

There was silence on the other end of the phone, except for laboured breathing. The words were forced out between gasps for breath. 'Just leave Felicity Paradise alone.'

13

They were home at last; the journey seemed to have gone on forever. Ellie had accepted a mug of soup and retired to Felicity's spare room. Before leaving for London, Felicity had had the foresight to tidy away her father's things, change the sheets and make the room look as anonymous as possible. Ellie looked exhausted. Felicity just hoped she would sleep. She telephoned Mel to say she was home, but Mel was asleep and Martin assured her that all was well, Charlie was thriving, Minty was happy and not to worry about them for the moment. Then she rang Annie who promised to drop Harvey around in the morning and confirmed that her constant checking had produced not a sign of Simon. Felicity made herself a cup of tea and went and sat out on her balcony. The sky was overcast but the town below her still looked very beautiful. The heavy cloud had warmed up the temperature so that it was balmy and there was no wind. She glanced at her watch; it was half past nine. She longed to be able to talk to Keith, to find out what had happened during the day, but didn't dare ring him now he'd be at home.

On cue her mobile vibrated in her jacket pocket. She took it out and stared in disbelief at the screen; he had to be telepathic. 'Keith?'

'Hello,' said Keith, 'how are things going?'

'Alright I suppose, you haven't heard anything, found anything?'

'Not really,' said Keith. 'That's what I'm ringing about, to give you a progress report.'

'Where are you, still at work?'

'No, I made my excuses after supper, said I needed a breath of fresh air to clear my head which was no more nor less than the truth. I'm afraid we've drawn an absolute blank so far. We've checked out likely cottage rentals, we've done door to door all around your cottage and I've circulated all the newspapers both down here and in Oxford. There will be an item about Simon on Spotlight tomorrow. I didn't do it today because I was worried Ellie might see it before you'd had a chance to explain things to her.'

'You are a nice man,' said Felicity.

'It's kind of you to say so, but I don't think I am really. I feel I should have taken you seriously earlier and launched the search for Simon Carter sooner. The trouble is, it's just not police policy but I should have had more sense and trusted your instincts.'

'Keith, wherever he is I don't think starting your

search twenty-four hours earlier would have made much difference.'

'I hope you're right,' said Keith. 'Now look, I think it's time I interviewed you formally and also Ellie. I'll do it myself rather than risk someone being totally insensitive with the poor girl. Could I come over tomorrow morning?'

'Yes, of course.'

'About ten?'

'Fine,' said Felicity, 'we'll be here.'

'There's just one thing I'll tell you now because I'd rather not discuss it at the moment in front of Ellie.'

'What?' said Felicity. 'What have you found out?'

'Nothing, but I have talked to the harbourmaster and to the fishermen around St Ives. If Simon had jumped into the water almost anywhere – off the pier, even off Man's Head Rock – initially his body would probably sink but it wouldn't leave the bay – chances are they would have found it by now. Somebody jumped off the pier a few months ago, I don't know if you remember? They found the body within hours at Bamaluz Beach as soon as the tide went out. He literally had travelled no more than a few yards from where he jumped.'

'So that's good news, isn't it?' said Felicity.

'Well, in a way, yes, but I thought it was probably not the sort of detail you'd like me to discuss with Ellie.'

'No, no, of course not. Thanks, and thank you for ringing, Keith.'

'No problem,' said Keith, 'and I'll see you in the morning.'

Betty Hill was late for work which was most unusual. Her teenage son, Mark, was becoming more and more of a handful and this morning he had refused utterly to get up and go to college. By the time they had finished arguing, not only had Mark missed his college bus but Betty had missed hers. He had been a lovely little boy, Mark, such a comfort to her when her husband had run off in rather a clichéd way with a barmaid from their local pub; she and Mark had been such a team. Now, though, the surly, foul-mouthed young man he had become was almost unrecognisable from her little chum through the years. Her friend Rachel said he was probably smoking dope and certainly his room smelt funny sometimes, but how to tackle it, how to stop it? It was Saturday tomorrow. She would have to sit him down and talk it all through; things couldn't go on as they were.

On reaching her office, she hurriedly took off her coat. The phone began to ring but she ignored it. Knocking gently on her boss's door, she opened it and went in. The room smelt heavily of alcohol and she saw that a bottle of whisky had toppled over and had soaked into the carpet. For a moment she thought he wasn't there and then she saw one chubby hand on the floor poking out from behind the desk. She ran round the side of the desk. Adam Dakin lay on his back, his mouth open, his eyes staring. He seemed to be reaching out across the carpet for something and Betty saw it was his nebuliser, just beyond the grasp of his outstretched hand. She looked at the scene for a moment, trying to absorb what had happened. Her brain, initially numb with shock, began to function again and as it did so Betty began to scream.

Chief Inspector Keith Penrose arrived at Jericho Cottage promptly at ten o'clock the following morning. Felicity ran down the stairs to answer the door and found him standing on the doorstep resplendent in one of his newer suits complete with a grey silk tie.

'Good morning, Chief Inspector,' she said, 'you look very smart this morning,' and then seeing Jack Curnow standing behind him, added, 'and you too sergeant.'

'Thank you Mrs Paradise,' said Jack, 'though obviously I can't compete with the boss when it comes to style.' They both smiled indulgently at Keith.

'Enough,' he said, 'I will not have you two ganging up on me.'

'Come on up and I'll make some coffee. Ellie has just had a shower; she'll be with us in five minutes.'

The three of them were sitting around the

kitchen table when Ellie came up the stairs. Both men stood up.

'I'm Chief Inspector Keith Penrose,' Keith said, extending a hand towards Ellie. 'And this is Sergeant Jack Curnow.'

Ellie smiled slightly at them both and shook hands.

'Coffee?' Felicity asked.

'Yes please, Fizzy,' Ellie said in a small voice. She sat down next to Keith who was studying her unobtrusively. Her colouring was amazing, bright red hair, stunning green eyes and a pale skin. She had strong features and at the moment was a little overweight, but beneath the puppy fat, Keith suspected there was a lovely bone structure. This was someone who was going to grow into herself. One day soon, she would be a very handsome woman, maybe even beautiful. At the moment though, she looked shy, uncomfortable and unbearably sad. His heart bled for her.

'Ellie,' Keith began, 'may I call you Ellie?'

'Yes, of course.'

'We've come to interview you today, Jack and I, not because in any way you or Mrs Paradise are a suspect with regard to your father's disappearance. It is simply that we're hoping that by talking to you both, it might assist in our investigation in some way. We can interview you separately if you'd prefer or together, it's entirely up to you.'

'Oh together please,' said Ellie. 'Is that alright Fizzy?'

'Of course,' said Felicity; she leant out and gave Ellie's hand a squeeze.

'Then we'll start with you, Mrs Paradise. Can you describe exactly the last time you saw Simon Carter and what made you believe that he had gone missing?'

Felicity described the events of Monday night, the omelette they had shared and then the call from Martin asking her to babysit Minty while Mel went to hospital, of the suggestion that Simon should come too and then the discarded coffee cup and newspaper the following day. 'I knew really something was wrong,' said Felicity, 'the first time I returned to the house, although it was perfectly logical that he had gone out for a walk. I was distracted though because I had Minty with me and so I wasn't thinking clearly enough.'

'Why?' asked Keith.

'Why what?'

'Why did you think he hadn't simply gone out?'

Felicity frowned with concentration. 'It was his fountain pen,' she said at last. 'It hadn't got the cap on, the ink would have dried up. It's not the sort of thing Simon would do, leave his pen uncapped.' She looked across to Ellie for confirmation. Ellie nodded her head vigorously. 'He's a very tidy man,' Felicity continued, 'and he loves that pen, he's had it for years. It was an engagement present from Ellie's

182

mother. In fact, I remember trailing round Oxford with her trying to find just the right one.'

'But there was no sign of a struggle,' Jack said, 'no overturned chair or no sign of a break-in?'

'Absolutely not.'

'So if your kidnap theory is correct, Mrs Paradise, Simon Carter must have known his kidnapper and must have let him into the house?'

'Or,' said Keith, 'maybe someone called him and asked to meet him outside the cottage, made it sound urgent – hence he left without capping his pen.' Keith paused. 'I know he didn't take his passport because we have that. Did he take his wallet because we could put a trace on his credit cards?'

'No,' said Felicity, 'his wallet is still here.'

'And his phone?'

'That's missing.'

'While I talk to Ellie,' Keith addressed them both, 'would you mind if Jack had a look through Mr Carter's things?'

Felicity deferred to Ellie. 'Ellie?'

'No, that's fine, anything that will help to find him.'

Felicity showed Jack downstairs to the spare room where she had packed Simon's things away into a box in the bottom of the wardrobe. 'There's this box,' she said, 'and there are just a few of his clothes which I've pushed to the back of the wardrobe here. I probably should have left his things as they were but

I couldn't bear it for Ellie – I don't have another room for her to sleep in.'

'That's fine,' said Jack, 'poor young woman, so soon after losing her mother.'

Keith and Ellie were deep in conversation when Felicity went back upstairs. She silently refilled their coffee mugs as they talked. Keith was so good with the young, she thought. Ellie had visibly relaxed; Keith's manner was avuncular and gentle.

'So you last spoke to your father on Sunday morning,' Keith was saying.

Ellie nodded.

'How did he seem?'

'Well, you know, we're both pretty sad at the moment.'

'Of course,' said Keith.

'But he was as jolly as one could expect. He and Fizzy were planning a walk, they were going to Zennor, that's right, isn't it, Fizzy?'

Felicity nodded.

'But the weather didn't turn out too good and so he was hoping you would allow him an alternative date with the Sunday papers, Fizzy.'

'I'm afraid that's what happened,' said Felicity, smiling.

'Did you make any plans to meet?' Keith asked.

'Yes, I was always coming down this weekend. I had planned to travel on my own to Cornwall today but then Fizzy said she was going to be in London and why not travel down together. So, I caught the train to King's Cross instead and came down last night instead of today.'

'How long are you, were you, planning to stay?'

'I was planning just to stay for the weekend but now obviously I will stay until we find him.'

There was a pause. 'You are at university I understand?' Keith said.

'Yes, at Edinburgh,' Ellie said. 'But I can't go back, couldn't study, not while my father is missing.'

'No, no, I understand that,' said Keith. 'We really are doing our very best to find him.'

'I'm sure you are,' said Ellie.

'One thought,' said Keith. 'Did you get as far as planning what train you would be travelling on today?'

'Yes,' said Ellie. 'Just after 6.30 at St Erth. Dad said he would pick me up.'

'It might be an idea if one of us met that train.'

'What are you thinking?' Felicity asked.

'If his grief had got too much for him, if being alone that night made him feel he had to get away for whatever reason, then the date with his daughter might just bring him back. He promised to meet her train. If he has disappeared of his own free will then meeting that train could be the trigger that makes him reappear.'

'How clever of you,' said Felicity.

'Not really,' said Keith, 'and I have to say that I don't think it's very likely that he'll be there, but I think it's worth pursuing. Would you like me to send someone?'

'No,' said Ellie. 'Absolutely not, we'll do it, won't we Fizzy?'

Felicity nodded. 'Yes.'

'Call me on my mobile when you've met the train,' Keith said.

Jack appeared at the top of the stairs and shook his head at Keith. 'Nothing there that's any help, sir.'

Keith sighed. 'A pity. So you're saying, Mrs Paradise, that as far as you are aware, apart from the man himself, the only things that are missing are his laptop and his phone.'

'I can't think of anything else,' Felicity said.

Keith stood up. 'We won't keep you any longer. It was very nice to meet you, Ellie and I'm sorry that it's under these circumstances.' He shook Ellie's hand and took off down the stairs. At the bottom of the stairs he said. 'Jack, can you fetch the car and drive down to the pier. I want to have another word with the harbourmaster before leaving town.' With Jack gone, Keith turned to Felicity. 'Do you feel like a walk down to the pier?'

'I do,' said Felicity, 'but I don't want to leave Ellie, not at the moment.'

Keith nodded. 'I understand.'

'Thank you for being so kind to her. You're very

186

good at your job, aren't you?'

Keith gave a heavy sigh and a small sad smile. 'I think we'd better withhold judgement on that until we find Simon Carter, don't you?'

14

Barbara Penrose was sitting at the kitchen table when Keith returned from work that evening. She wore the expression which over the years he had come to dread. It meant he had done something seriously wrong though for the life of him on this occasion, he could not imagine what it could be.

'Had a good day?' he asked, deciding to ignore the deep frown and accusing eyes. 'I'm going to have a glass of wine, would you like one?'

'No, thank you,' said Barbara. 'I've just been watching you on Spotlight.'

'Would you like my autograph?' Keith asked, in a pathetic attempt at humour.

'That man who is missing, Simon ...'

'Simon Carter,' Keith said.

'He's the same man who was with Felicity Paradise the day we had lunch at Porthminster?'

'That's right,' said Keith, cheerfully, 'how clever of you to remember.'

Barbara was clearly unimpressed by his attempt

at flattery. 'You're making rather a fuss, aren't you, about a missing person. People go missing all the time, so you tell me. Why are you so concerned about this one? Is it because he is a friend of Mrs Paradise?'

Keith made much of pouring his wine and replacing the bottle in the fridge, giving him time to think. He turned around and met Barbara's eye. 'In a way, yes,' he admitted. 'Mrs Paradise thinks his life is in danger, she is usually right about that sort of thing and so I've decided I should take his disappearance seriously.'

'Very seriously, for him to be on Spotlight. Have you been seeing much of Mrs Paradise then?'

'I interviewed her and the missing man's daughter this morning in St Ives,' Keith said, 'and other than that, I met her in Malpas a week or two ago when she first expressed concern about the situation in which Mr Carter found himself in.'

'And what situation is that exactly?' Barbara asked.

'It's fairly dreary, it's all about banking. Do you really want to know?'

'Yes, I do,' said Barbara, 'and I will have a glass of wine.'

'In a nutshell,' said Keith, as he poured Barbara's wine, 'Simon Carter has some dubious insider knowledge about a Bank which is hoping to attract some Government support. There are billions of pounds at stake apparently. Mrs Paradise is worried that the information Mr Carter has could jeopardise the deal and therefore his position is a dangerous one.'

'Mrs Paradise lives in a different world than the rest of us,' Barbara said, icily.

'Possibly,' said Keith.

Barbara sipped her wine thoughtfully. 'Is the name of the bank Carlyon by any chance?'

'Yes,' said Keith, surprised, 'how on earth did you know that?'

'They've just been on the news, it was the main item on the six o'clock news. They've had to have a Government bail-out to keep them going. I gather we taxpayers now own a part of the Bank but, of course, nobody asked us first.'

'Hang on a moment,' said Keith. 'You're saying that the deal with Carlyon has gone through?'

'Yes.'

'Where's the remote control?'

'On the side there,' said Barbara.

Keith flashed through the channels until he found News 24. The story being discussed was the loss of two more soldiers in Afghanistan but the strip running along the bottom of the screen told the story – Government bail-out for Carlyon Bank.

'So it looks like Mrs Paradise was wrong,' said Barbara, triumphantly.

Or right, thought Keith, which means that either Simon Carter is going to reappear in the next few hours or he is already dead.

While Keith and Barbara Penrose were drinking wine in their kitchen, Felicity and Ellie were standing forlornly on Platform One at St Erth station. The London train had come and gone and there was no sign of Simon. They clambered wearily back over the bridge to Felicity's car.

'We could wait a few minutes if you like,' Felicity said, 'he could have got the train time wrong.'

Ellie shook her head; she was close to tears. 'No point Fizzy, let's just go home.'

Felicity made them a hot chicken salad which should have been delicious but neither of them was hungry. Ellie barely touched hers.

'I think I'll go to bed,' Ellie said.

'It's only half past eight, will you sleep?'

'I've got a book,' said Ellie, 'I'll try and read that.'

As soon as Ellie was out of earshot, Felicity rang Mel. She had been putting off ringing all day expecting some harsh words from her daughter and she was not disappointed.

'Where have you been?' Mel said. 'Are you ever going to come and see your new grandson again?

'Don't start Mel,' said Felicity, wearily. 'You know where I've been. I've been to London, I've come back with Ellie and we spent this morning being interviewed by the police. This evening, we've been to meet the train that Ellie would have been on in the vain hope that maybe Simon would be there to meet it.'

'And was he?'

'No,' said Felicity.

'So what about popping around to see us now?' Mel said. 'Charlie has decided that day is night and night is day so there would be no problem about seeing him now, he seems to be awake most of the night.'

'Poor you,' said Felicity, 'it is tough, isn't it?'

'Well, are you coming over?' said Mel.

'No,' said Felicity, 'not tonight, I'm not going to leave Ellie.'

'She's not a child, Mum.'

'I know,' said Felicity, 'and I'm really sorry Mel, but I'm not prepared to leave her alone at the minute with her father missing – it is an awful situation.'

'There is no need to explain it to me,' said Mel, 'I know all about it. My father didn't just go missing, he died.'

'But you still have your mother,' said Felicity.

'Do I?' Mel replied and the phone went dead.

Felicity looked helplessly at the phone in her hand. Should she ring her back? Probably not, they would both only say things they would regret later. Was she doing the right thing, favouring the needs of Gilla's daughter over her own?

She was still standing uncertainly over the telephone when the doorbell rang, making her jump. She looked at her watch, it was well after nine. Who on earth? Perhaps it was Simon. She started down the stairs but even as she ran, she remembered that he had a key.

Ellie appeared at her bedroom door, bleary-eyed in her nightdress.

'Was that the doorbell?'

'Yes,' said Felicity, as she rushed past her to open the front door. 'But it won't be Dad because Dad has a key.' She unlatched the door to find Keith standing on the pavement outside. 'Keith,' she said, 'have you got any news?'

He shook his head. 'Not about Simon I'm afraid, no.'

'But you have some news?'

'Yes, can I come in?'

'Sorry, sorry,' said Felicity. 'Come on in.' Felicity led the way upstairs followed by Keith and Ellie, struggling into a dressing gown.

'I take it that the trip to St Erth produced no results?' Keith asked.

'No,' said Felicity, 'but what is your news?'

'Carlyon has been bailed out by the Government, the deal is done and it is now partly owned by us, the taxpayers. The board of directors remains the same, Hugh Randall is staying on as Chairman.'

Ellie looked from one to the other of them. 'What does that mean?' she said, 'what does that mean for Dad?'

'It means,' said Keith, 'that he is no longer a threat to Carlyon, assuming of course that he ever was.'

'Surely even at this late stage he could unseat the deal if he told them what he knew?' Felicity suggested.

'I very much doubt it,' said Keith. 'I think everyone would close ranks. The Government would look extremely stupid if they were seen to have backed a fraudulent bank. It is in nobody's interest, not the Government's, not the Bank's, not the investors'. This deal has to go ahead now.'

'So wasn't that always the case?' Felicity asked.

'You could argue so, yes, but while the Carlyon board were still trying to persuade the Chancellor to do the deal, they were obviously very vulnerable.'

'But no matter how bad things were, the Government couldn't have let the bank go bust, could they?' Felicity said.

'Look what happened to Lehmans,' Keith replied, 'it seems at the moment anything is possible.'

'So,' said Ellie, 'if we are right about Daddy being kidnapped, they will let him go now, won't they?'

Keith smiled at her. 'In theory, yes.'

'Would you like a drink,' said Felicity, 'glass of wine, or something?'

'No I'd better not, I've had one already this evening and I'm driving. Cup of tea would be good though.'

'Ellie?'

'No thanks,' said Ellie, 'I think I'll go back to bed.'

'Are you alright, darling?' Felicity asked.

'Yes, it's good news, isn't it?'

'I think so,' said Felicity. 'Assuming, of course, that Daddy's disappearance is linked to Carlyon, the problem is we just don't know.'

'What do you really think, Keith?' Felicity asked when Ellie was out of earshot. She had put the kettle on the Aga and was leaning against the warmth of the rail for comfort.

Keith came and stood close behind her. 'I don't know, it could be good news, I suppose.'

'But you don't think so, do you?' said Felicity.

'I am concerned for Mr Carter's safety,' he replied, formally. 'I had a conversation with the Hong Kong police today. They are treating Alex Button's death as murder of course, hard not to really when the poor bloke has a bullet in the head. They have no leads, no witnesses, nothing to go on, though they do believe it could be linked in some way to his dismissal from Carlyon.'

'Oh Keith, I can't bear it for Ellie,' Felicity covered her eyes. I must not cry, she thought. She felt Keith's hands on her shoulders; he turned her around gently and took her in his arms. The relief was enormous, all the tensions of the last few days drained away. She no longer felt the need to cry, she was being comforted and she felt safe, protected and cherished.

She slipped her arms around him and they stood together for some long time until the insistence of the kettle made them break away. Flustered, Felicity began making tea. 'Finding no body is good news, it keeps hope alive.'

'I rechecked at the Harbour Office this morning. If he drowned anywhere in the Bay we'll have a floater by the middle of next week, the coastguards are all alerted,' said Keith.

'A floater, please!' said Felicity, horrified.

'Sorry, not my words, one of the fisherman's.'

'And if not?'

'We'll just keep trying; it's all we can do. I can't even say to you that we will keep trying until the trail goes cold, because there isn't a trail. What slightly concerns me is that Hong Kong believes Alex Button's death was a highly professional job. Taking anyone out in central Hong Kong is no easy matter, apparently. Simon's disappearance is also very professional. There was over three hundred pounds of cash in his wallet, I don't know if you were aware of that? It was left untouched, the house and contents undamaged. One can only hope that whoever killed Alex Button didn't make his next port of call St Ives.'

Felicity handed Keith his cup of tea and they both sat down.

'I don't know what to do with Ellie. I'm finding this waiting awful, so God knows what it is like for her.'

'You're here for her, that's what really matters.'

'But even that's not easy,' said Felicity, 'I'm getting an awful lot of stick from Mel. With a new baby, she needs her mum.'

'She's got a mother,' said Keith, 'Ellie hasn't.'

'That's what I said, but it didn't cut much ice.'

Keith smiled at Felicity. 'She's a bit of a bully, your Mel, isn't she?'

Felicity nodded, miserably.

'Look,' said Keith, 'young Charlie has years ahead of him to be spoilt by his Granny. Right now, you've got your priorities right but maybe tomorrow you could compromise and both spend the day with Mel. If you give me her telephone number as a back-up to your mobile, I'll let you know the moment I have any news. To be with the children might be good for both of you, rather than sitting around here.'

'I think we both feel we want to be here in case he turns up.'

'Then leave him a note.'

'He might have lost his key.'

'Then pin the note to the door.'

'You're right,' said Felicity, 'as usual.'

Keith smiled at her. 'Can I have that in writing, Mrs Paradise?'

'Certainly not,' said Felicity.

Keith was in no hurry to get home as he drove along the darkened A30. It had needed the very

197

extremes of willpower not to kiss her when he had held her in his arms. He also knew if he had done so he would never have been able to let her go. He was walking a tightrope and he was starting to wonder whether it was affecting his marriage. Clearly, Barbara had her suspicions, which of course were not without foundation. In Felicity, Keith felt he had found his soulmate. They just fitted together – mentally, emotionally and, he suspected, physically, they were two halves of a whole. A wave of longing swept over him so forcefully that he gasped out loud, gripped the steering wheel and slowed the car to a funereal pace.

This had to stop. As a child, his weekly trips to Chapel and his parents' strong moral code had formed the fabric of his young life. As a man, he had witnessed enough human misery to know that society needed rules and that rules needed to be obeyed. Marriages within the police force were notoriously tricky and he and Barbara had done well to stay together. Through the years, she had deeply resented his commitment to his job, particularly when the children were small. Ever a sensible and practical woman though, she had found a solution. Her work for the local council totally absorbed her, and so they were on an equal footing now, both committed to their jobs, and it suited them. He liked her, he respected her; her lack of humour was a constant sadness but she was a good woman who deserved a faithful husband. When had love died? He wondered if he had ever loved her; certainly he had never felt about her as he did now for Felicity Paradise. Did Barbara love him? It was hard to tell. Their lives were bound together by the minutiae of domestic arrangements: children, friends, routines.

He needed to be so careful about keeping his feelings in check. Felicity was very vulnerable at the moment. She had just lost her best friend, Simon Carter was missing, and she had twin responsibilities for both Ellie and her daughter with her new baby. She was doing a great deal of caring and she had no one to care for her – how he longed to fill that role.

He reached Chiverton Cross roundabout and turned off towards Truro, slowing his pace still more to give himself time to think before reaching home. To take advantage of Felicity's vulnerability at this moment would be truly appalling. He felt as if he was looking over the edge of a precipice. Once this particular crisis was over and Simon Carter was found, he would have to distance himself from her, it was the only solution. The pain of such a thought almost took his breath away. He was not used to these violent swings of emotion. He turned down Lemon Street, heading towards home. The spires of the Cathedral, so familiar and normally so reassuring, were ahead of him. For some reason the sight of the Cathedral bought a lump to his throat. God, he was a mess. Suddenly he knew he couldn't face going home. He turned right and headed out to the ring road. He would go back to his office for an hour or so and try to clear his head.

Moments later he pulled into the car park, shut off the engine and sat with his forehead resting on the steering wheel for a moment. Whatever name you gave these feelings he had for Felicity, these mind-numbing, stomach-churning feelings, he knew they were not of a temporary nature, he was stuck with them. In a moment of terrifying clarity, he realised he was going to love Felicity Paradise for the rest of his life.

15

The days flowed one into another. In the immediate aftermath of the Carlyon bail-out, both Felicity and Ellie were on red alert. In a state of heightened tension, every time there were footsteps outside the cottage, they tensed; every time the phone rang they ran to it in panic. However, as one day followed another and there was still no sign of Simon, they slipped into a state of apathy, their situation becoming almost surreal, their lives in limbo. They had developed a routine which revolved around Mel and her children. They went over to Hayle after breakfast each day, staying for the day to help and returning to Jericho Cottage immediately after bath time. The children were their lifeline and Mel, having calmed down, was kind and considerate to Ellie.

Keith Penrose kept in daily touch. Realising that every time he rang he was going to spread panic throughout the household, he suggested that he made a routine call every day between five and six and that he would only ring at any other time of the day if there had been any developments. After what was now nearly two weeks, any developments seemed likely to signify a body.

At night Felicity would replay again and again the last hour or so she had spent with Simon, trying to convince herself that there was some clue in his behaviour as to his disappearance; that perhaps everything had got too much for him and he had simply gone away for a while. She tried very hard to convince herself that this could be the case, but she just knew that it was not. They had been cross with one another that last night and conversation during supper had been strained. News of Alex Button's death had obviously been a shock to Simon but he had seemed anxious to play it down. Was he bluffing, had he really thought it was safest for all concerned if he took himself off and went into hiding until the Carlyon deal was done? That was possible, but if he had decided to do so surely he would have told her what he was doing. It was inconceivable that he would simply disappear, knowing the anxiety and misery he would cause. He was not a particularly imaginative man, but he was certainly a kind one. Gilla's death had devastated him but not felled him. Whichever way she turned it, however she looked at it, she was absolutely certain that Simon Carter would not have walked out of their lives of his own free will.

The call came at two o'clock, two weeks and a

day after Simon's disappearance. The household were all taking a nap, except for Felicity. Ellie was sleeping very badly at night and had slipped into the habit of having an after-lunch nap with the children, as did Mel. Felicity was in Mel's garden with a wheelbarrow and secateurs trying to tidy it up for the autumn. Potentially it was a beautiful garden, a long strip which ran down to the very edge of the estuary – but just as builders' wives can never get a new bathroom and doctors' wives receive absolutely no sympathy however ill they may be, so gardeners' wives have to accept that their own garden will always look like a jungle. Felicity paused in her work to watch a flock of Canada geese flying up the estuary – had they just arrived, she wondered? They flew strongly in perfect formation, a wonderful sight. The phone rang; she fumbled in her pocket, pulled it out and fear immediately gripped her when she saw that the call was from Keith.

'Where are you?' he asked.

'In the garden.'

'Alone?'

'Yes.' She knew what was coming.

'A body has been washed up on the beach at Newquay, it could be Simon.'

'Oh God,' said Felicity, 'have you seen the body, does it look like him?'

'There's no easy way to put this,' said Keith, 'all we can tell you about the body is that it is male. The crabs have been at it, there's one hand missing and no feet. There is no possibility of making any sort of visual identification and I think the best way forward would be a DNA.'

'You think it's him, don't you?' Felicity said, in a small voice.

'I think it could be,' said Keith, 'I certainly think you need to prepare yourself and Ellie for the possibility that it is Simon. We have no recent unsolved male missing persons in the area at the moment – we have missing persons going back years of course, but nobody current, except Simon.'

'So what do we do?' Felicity asked, shakily.

'I've been trying to think how to make this as easy as possible for Ellie. I've made an appointment down at Stennack Surgery for four o'clock this afternoon. If you could take her down there they will do a DNA right away and I've got a car coming to pick it up.'

'How long will it take to get a result? This is a nightmare, Keith.'

'Only a few days, the chap doing the autopsy is a pal of mine, I'm going to lean on him, explain the situation.'

'Thanks Keith,' said Felicity, her voice full of gratitude, 'what on earth would we do without you?'

Keith pocketed his phone and climbed into the car beside Jack Curnow. He stared out of the window.

The body, or what there was of it, was being stretchered up to the waiting ambulance; the tide was out, the sun was shining. With most of the visitors gone now, Fistral beach had never looked more lovely, but for this gruesome discovery the sea had thrown up. Keith had spared Felicity too much detail. The body had got caught in a piece of fishing net which had made it easier for the crabs to do their work. It was only just possible to see that the remains were human.

'How did she take it?' Jack asked.

'Well, you know Mrs Paradise, she was stalwart. She is going to take Ellie down to the surgery for four o'clock. I want to get these results as quickly as possible. Let's go back to Truro, Jack.'

Jack slipped the car into gear and began to drive along the front. 'Why did the body end up here, sir? Do you think he was in Newquay all the time?'

Keith shook his head. 'I'm going to talk to the coastguards and the St Ives harbourmaster again, but I think two weeks is about right for a body to travel from St Ives to Newquay. There is a problem, though.'

'Which is?' Jack asked.

'I think I told you that we have established that if Simon Carter had jumped or been pushed into the sea anywhere around St Ives, his body would never have left the Bay.'

'So the significance is, sir, that dead or alive Simon was put in a boat and taken out of the Bay and dumped at sea somewhere beyond Seal Island. That's the only way his body could have ended up in Newquay. Is that right?'

'In which case,' Keith concluded, 'this is no accident, this is murder, but God knows how we ever prove it.'

Ellie remained calm and controlled while the nurse took the swab. Then she and Felicity walked from Stennack Surgery down into the town, bought the ingredients from the Co-op to make a shepherd's pie and walked the short distance back to Jericho Cottage. Keith rang soon after their return at his usual time.

'We've done the DNA,' Felicity said.

'How is she?'

Felicity glanced across the room. Ellie was sitting out on the balcony with a cup of tea. Felicity walked through to her sitting room so she was out of earshot. 'Very composed, as always, too composed. I wish she would howl and scream and cry.'

'If you want to leave this until the morning, it's fine,' said Keith, 'but I was wondering if there were any distinguishing marks on Simon. He doesn't sound the right sort of chap for one but does he have a tattoo, or maybe some sort of injury or any permanent jewellery, a wedding ring that sort of thing?'

'How long are you in the office?' Felicity asked.

'Another half hour I suppose,' said Keith.

'I'll call you back.'

Felicity walked through to the balcony and sat down beside Ellie.

'That was Keith on the phone, he was wondering whether there was anything we could think of that might help him identify whether the body is Daddy's or not.'

Ellie seemed to be in a trance. She dragged her eyes away from staring into the middle distance and looked at Felicity. 'What sort of thing?'

'He wore a signet ring, didn't he?'

'Yes,' said Ellie, 'on his left hand, it's a pair of crossed swords, some sort of family emblem but I've never been sure what.'

'And any kind of injury?'

'He wasn't sporty, was he?' said Ellie.

'So no cauliflower ears,' said Felicity, with a small smile which was returned. 'Did he have any operations or anything like that?' she asked gently.

'I know he had his appendix out when he was a boy.'

'That might help I suppose,' said Felicity, 'I'll pass it on. Anything else?'

'I don't think so,' said Ellie.

Felicity put her hand on her arm. 'I'll just go and ring Keith back and tell him what you've told me.'

'OK,' said Ellie, her eyes once more fixed on the horizon.

It was only as Felicity was walking into the

sitting room to dial Keith's number, she realised that they had been talking about Simon entirely in the past tense.

'Not much to go on, I'm afraid,' said Felicity, 'he had his appendix out as a boy so I suppose there would be a small scar and obviously no visual appendix, but he did wear a signet ring.'

'Which hand?' Keith asked.

'Left.'

'Damn, that's the one which is missing.'

'Oh don't, Keith,' Felicity said, feeling her stomach heave.

'I'm sorry, I'm so sorry,' said Keith, 'I am trying to spare you as much of the detail of this as I can.'

'I know you are,' said Felicity, 'and thank you. The signet ring – if you do find the other hand – is gold with crossed swords engraved on it.'

'And a watch?' Keith asked.

'He has a gold watch too,' said Felicity, remembering, 'with a …' she frowned, 'black leather strap, it could be grey but I think it's black. A very standard watch with proper hands, not digital. He often didn't wear it though, I suppose because he was down here with no business meetings and swimming a lot. It was always lying about on the bathroom shelf.'

'But it's not there now?' said Keith.

'No, no it isn't.'

'So chances are he was wearing it?'

'I suppose so. Keith?'

'Yes,' said Keith gently.

'We're all talking about him in the past. I've just realised Ellie and I have had a whole conversation talking about him as if he was dead.'

'It is so difficult to know what to say to you,' Keith said, 'I don't want to give you false hope, on the other hand I don't want you to abandon hope altogether.'

'Will you call off the search for him now, now this body has been found?'

'No, the Missing Persons Unit are still on it,' said Keith, 'and a flood of people are coming forward and claiming the body belongs to a relation of theirs. This always happens when someone unidentified is found, it opens old cases.'

'But you're only making the comparison with Ellie's DNA?'

'At the moment, yes,' said Keith.

'That means you're pretty certain it's Simon.'

'I suppose I am,' Keith admitted.

Felicity made shepherd's pie while Ellie remained on the balcony. She poured them both a hefty glass of wine and coaxed Ellie in for supper. Neither of them were hungry but they made an attempt at it.

'So how long until we get the results?' Ellie asked as they were sitting over their wine. She sounded so weary, like an old woman.

'About a week, as I understand it,' said Felicity, 'Keith is going to tell us definitely tomorrow when to expect them.'

'He's very kind, isn't he?' said Ellie, looking at Felicity for the first time all evening.

'Yes, he is.'

'Mum was always teasing you about him, wasn't she?' Ellie said, with a small smile.

'Yes she was, but he is a happily married man, Ellie, so don't you start.'

'But he's also a good friend and a good policeman. This would have been even worse without him,' Ellie said.

'Yes it would,' Felicity agreed, with a sigh.

There seemed nothing else to do but continue in the same routine. Felicity suggested that perhaps she and Ellie should go away for a few days but Ellie wanted to stay in St Ives.

'The body might not be Daddy's,' she said, in a rare moment of hope, 'in which case we need to stay around here in case he turns up.'

'I'm not sure who's helping who,' Felicity said to Mel, while they were washing up companionably in the kitchen. Ellie was out in the garden with Minty, Charlie asleep in his pram.

'You and Ellie have been great,' Mel said, 'I don't know how I would have managed without you. I am sorry I was so grumpy – hormones, I suppose.'

'That's OK, I think you've all helped us far more than we've helped you,' said Felicity. 'The only time Ellie seems to be functioning at the moment is when she is playing with Minty. The rest of the time, poor love, she is walking around like a zombie. I try to talk to her in the evenings but she just shuts off.'

'There is nothing to say, that's the trouble,' said Mel. 'Until these results come through there are no words of comfort. When will you hear?'

'Next Monday, Keith reckons.'

'He's going to telephone you?'

'I suppose so,' said Felicity, 'I know he will let me know the minute he has any news.'

They dragged their way through the weekend. Ellie remained calm but monosyllabic, which worried Felicity enormously. Where was all this pent-up emotion being channelled and how would it manifest itself and when? On Monday morning Ellie was quieter than ever. Felicity woke up with a sense of dread in the pit of her stomach. They breakfasted and as usual drove over to Hayle.

'I don't know what time he'll ring,' Felicity said.

'When he's ready, I suppose,' Ellie replied, dismissively.

Keith sat opposite Horace Greenaway, frowning.

'And you are absolutely certain about this, Horace?'

'You know sometimes, Penrose, you can be quite astonishingly insulting.'

'I'm sorry, Horace,' said Keith, 'but this is really important.'

'It's always really important. Establishing the true identity of the dead is quite as important as establishing the true identity of the living – in fact, more so. This chap, whoever he may be, is not the father of Ellie Carter, so presumably therefore, he is not Simon Carter.'

'Can we double-check your findings in some way?'

'Keith, we've just conducted a DNA test, they are not father and daughter.'

'Do you have his dental records, I asked for them to be sent to you?'

'I believe so, yes,' said Horace.

'Well would you do me a favour then, Horace? Would you run a check on those? I need this to be a belt and braces job. As I mentioned to you, Ellie only lost her mother just over a month ago, I don't want to give her false hopes that her father may still be alive if he's not.'

'Penrose, how many times do I have to spell this out to you?'

'I know, I know,' Keith interrupted, 'the DNA is not a match, but there are two ways of looking at this, Horace. Either the body is not Simon Carter because his DNA does not match that of his daughter, or else, the body *is* Simon Carter and Ellie is not his daughter.'

16

She was in the garden hanging out some washing when she saw Keith. He obviously had abandoned his car out on the road or else Jack had dropped him off. He was walking slowly up the drive towards Mel's cottage, unaware that he was being watched. He walked slowly and, knowing him as she did, Felicity realised that he was a man bearing bad news. He had told her once that bringing news to a family, particularly unexpected news, of the death or serious injury of a loved one, was not only the hardest part of the job but the one element of it he could never shed. 'I file them neatly away,' he had said, 'but they keep popping back up, I never seem to be able to forget them.' 'Maybe it's your way of showing a mark of respect,' Felicity had suggested at the time. Now it was their turn.

Ellie was in the house. Felicity had an overriding desire to rush through the house and stop Keith before he reached them, anything to spare Ellie the news he had to tell them. Instead, she put down the washing, went back into the house and called Ellie's name.

'Keith's here, Ellie, presumably he has the news.'

Ellie joined her in the hall. They stared at one another and instinctively held hands. Ellie was very pale. Felicity opened the door just as Keith arrived. He gave them a wintry smile. 'You have news?' Felicity asked.

Keith nodded. 'Can I come in?'

'Of course.'

Minty was at playgroup. Above in the bedroom they could hear Charlie beginning to wail, indicating his requirement for another meal. Momentarily Felicity was relieved; it would keep Mel occupied. Instinctively she felt that she and Ellie needed to do this alone. She led Keith into the kitchen and the three of them sat down at the kitchen table.

Surprisingly it was Ellie who spoke first. 'It's him then, isn't it?' she said.

Keith looked extremely uncomfortable. Felicity frowned, what was going on? Keith cleared his throat. 'The body we've found is not a DNA match to you.'

Ellie's face lit up. 'You mean it's not Daddy? That's wonderful.' She turned to Felicity and grasped her hand. 'Fizzy, do you hear what he's saying? It's not Daddy.'

Keith still looked unaccountably sombre. 'Is that what you're saying, Keith?' Felicity asked.

'We're checking the dental records.' He turned to Ellie. 'We have your father's dental records and we're double-checking those. Until we've done that we can't be absolutely sure.'

Felicity stared at Keith. 'I don't understand what you're saying, Keith. I always thought that DNA was an absolute given, particularly between a child and its parent, a close relationship like that. Surely it's either a DNA match or it isn't and if it isn't, then they're not related and the body isn't Simon's.'

Keith was clearly struggling. 'That's true,' he said, 'but we still need proof as to who the body is and comparing the dental records will confirm this one way or another.'

There was a tense silence in the room, broken at last by Ellie's voice. 'He's saying that he still thinks the body belongs to Daddy, he just doesn't think that Daddy is my father.'

Felicity looked appalled. 'Is that what you're saying, Keith?'

Keith would not meet her eye. She could not remember seeing him more uncomfortable. 'Ellie is right, it is a possibility.'

'I don't know why you are reacting like this,' Felicity said, jumping up and starting to march around the room. 'Why on earth should you think that Simon isn't Ellie's father? You have a body which, which…,' she stumbled over the words, 'can't be easily identified so you go for DNA. DNA isn't a match so why isn't that the end of it, why don't you assume therefore that it is someone other than Simon

216

Carter? Suggesting to Ellie that Simon isn't her father is an unspeakably cruel thing to do.'

At last Keith raised anguished eyes but he looked at Ellie not at Felicity. 'I am desperately hoping that the dental records don't match, Ellie, but there are similarities that can't be ignored. The man was a similar height to your father and he had been in the water for the same length of time as your father has been missing.' He hesitated. 'We haven't been able to locate his left hand so the signet ring, or lack of it, is of no help. Don't think for a moment I'm suggesting that your father isn't your biological father but it's my duty and responsibility to do everything I can to correctly identify the man we pulled out of the sea at Newquay. Comparing the dental records will be the final piece in the jigsaw.'

'I understand,' said Ellie, in a small voice, 'really I do. It's OK.'

'I don't understand,' said Felicity ten minutes later as she was walking with Keith down the drive towards his car. 'I can't see why you should assume that the DNA is not enough. I can't see why you're prolonging this agony for Ellie. If the man you pulled out of the sea isn't her father, surely that's an end to it? I know you have to be very careful and follow the rules and procedures in trying to identify someone but to suggest to Ellie that Simon isn't her father, it's just too much on top of everything else.' Keith remained silent. 'Aren't you going to say anything?' Felicity asked belligerently.

Keith stopped. They were a few yards from his car but out of sight of the house now. 'It wouldn't be right,' Keith said, 'to tell Ellie the body we've found isn't Simon Carter until we are absolutely sure of our facts.'

Felicity was still angry. 'But to insinuate,' she began and then she looked at Keith's face. He was miserable, awkward. 'Is there something you're not telling me, Keith?'

He shook his head. 'No.'

'Then why are you putting us through this?'

Keith didn't answer for a moment, then he put his hands on Felicity's shoulders. 'I am sorry I'm not making this easy, but …'

'You believe the body you found is Simon Carter, don't you?'

'I don't know,' said Keith, 'but I do believe it could be.'

Ellie went to bed as soon as they got home to Jericho Cottage, wanting neither food nor drink. In desperation for someone to talk to Felicity rang Josh Buchanan. They had been in regular contact in the days that had followed Felicity's return to Cornwall with Ellie. She had found him a great comfort and he had promised to come down to Cornwall as soon as he had finished the rather tricky case he was involved with at the moment.

'Fizzy, what news?' he said, as soon as he heard her voice. For some reason Felicity felt an overriding desire to protect both Simon and Ellie, Gilla too, come to that.

'They're still checking, it's dental records now, we should have an answer tomorrow or Wednesday morning at the worst.'

'God it does drag on, what a nightmare. How is Ellie?'

'Well, you know, bearing up.'

'I've got some news for you actually,' said Josh, 'I was going to telephone you this evening in any event.'

'What's that?' Felicity asked.

'Adam Dakin is dead.'

'Dead! What, murdered?'

'No, no Fizzy, less dramatics please. He had an asthma attack in his office. It must have happened the day you saw him or the day after. I only picked up news of his death because there was an obituary in *The Times*.'

'Everyone dies who's connected with Carlyon.'

'Oh come on Fizz, that's a bit of an exaggeration, isn't it? How many thousands of people do they employ?'

Felicity ignored him. 'Alex Button, the potential whistle-blower in Hong Kong, Simon Carter the potential whistle-blower in the UK and then Adam

219

Dakin who I told about Simon's findings in Hong Kong.'

'Adam Dakin died of natural causes, Fizzy.'

'Are you sure?'

'As sure as I can be. If it had been murder there would have been a huge hue and cry. As it is, his death passed by unnoticed; it was only the obituary that made me aware of his death. Poor old Adam, I imagine the cause was probably just one meal too many. I was going to add plus being frightened by you, but I can see you're not in the mood for a joke.'

'No I'm not,' said Felicity, 'definite sense of humour loss at the moment.'

'Why not ask your policeman chum to check out the circumstances of Adam's death?'

'Good idea,' said Felicity, 'I will.'

It had been a lifetime's ambition for Bill and Betty Cole to retire to Cornwall. They had raised their two children in a semi-detached house on the outskirts of Blackburn. When the children were six and eight, they had managed to save up enough money to buy a caravan and each summer the four of them took the caravan down to Cornwall for three weeks. When the children became too old to accompany their parents on holiday, Bill and Betty had continued to come on their own and then on Bill's retirement, they had at last achieved their dream. They sold their house in Blackburn and bought a small bungalow in Newquay. Fate, however, at its most cruel, had intervened and within four months of settling into their new home, Betty was diagnosed with breast cancer and within a year she was dead. Bill was in a dilemma. After the initial shock, he had settled into a state of inertia. He had made a few friends in Newquay; there were a lot of retired people like him, but they were not lifelong friends. They were not people he had known since he was a boy who had raised their kids alongside his; there was no history, no depth to the relationships. One of his children had emigrated to Canada, but the other, his daughter, still lived near Blackburn. The sensible thing would be to return home: Blackburn would always be home. Their dream, his and Betty's, had turned to dust and yet the effort of moving again, of leaving the life that he and Betty had finally achieved after so many years of planning seemed wrong.

Bill was contemplating his predicament as he walked along the sand with his dog Bertie, a chocolate Labrador who had been Betty's pride and joy. He was lost in thought and it was some while before he took any notice of Bertie's excited barking. The dog was digging frantically in the sand where it was still wet from the receding tide.

'What are you doing, you silly dog?' Bill called. 'Come here, boy.'

Bertie lolloped over to Bill holding something in

his mouth, triumphant, very pleased with himself.

'What have you got there then?' Bill said, leaning down to take what the dog was offering him. Then seeing what it was, he recoiled in horror. In Bertie's mouth was a human hand, apparently torn from its body, and glinting in the sun on the hand's little finger was a signet ring.

The phone was already ringing as Keith entered his office the following morning. 'Penrose.'

'Keith, it's Felicity.'

'No news yet I'm afraid, in fact I've only just arrived.'

'No, no, that's not why I'm ringing,' said Felicity, 'I wondered if you could check out something for me?'

'What sort of thing?' Keith asked, searching desperately on his cluttered desk for a piece of paper on which to write.

'You remember I went up to Carlyon Bank the day I collected Ellie?'

'I do indeed,' said Keith.

'I saw a man called Adam Dakin, he was an old friend of my husband's.'

'I remember that too,' said Keith, 'and he blanked you by all accounts.'

'Yes, the thing is Keith, he's dead.'

'How? What happened?'

'Well that's just it, according to Josh Buchanan – you know, Charlie's partner?'

'Yes, I remember him.'

'Well according to Josh, Adam died of natural causes, an asthma attack, but I wondered if you could just check it out, just to make sure.'

'Is there any reason to suppose it should be anything different, unless, of course, you frightened him to death.'

Felicity let out a theatrical sigh. 'That's exactly what Josh said.'

'Obviously a very discerning man who knows you well,' said Keith.

'Keith, you have no idea what a relief it is just to have a conversation which doesn't revolve directly around Simon and the body on the beach.'

'It must be a terrible strain for you,' Keith said.

'Well, it's not pleasant for me,' said Felicity, 'but my troubles pale into insignificance compared with Ellie.' The thought of Ellie silenced them both for a moment.

'Are you saying you think this Adam Dakin was murdered like Alex Button in Hong Kong?'

'I don't know,' said Felicity, 'but it would be good to check it out.'

'I'll do that,' said Keith, 'and come back to you. I'll also let you know the moment we have any news from the lab.'

Keith was back to her within an hour.

'The Met were able to confirm that Adam Dakin

died of natural causes,' Keith said. 'The pathologist in charge of the case says the man was so unfit, so overweight and with so many failing organs, to write an accurate cause of death would have involved a saga of several hundred pages. As far as cause of death is concerned, he said it was a question of "take your pick".'

'He was very overweight and very short of breath,' Felicity conceded, 'and a very nasty colour, too.'

'So it doesn't look like we can blame Carlyon for his death,' said Keith.

'No, perhaps not,' said Felicity, 'thanks for checking it out. No news from the lab?'

'No news,' said Keith.

The hand arrived at Horace Greenaway's laboratory just after three o'clock in the afternoon. Keith arrived ten minutes later.

'So?' said Keith, struggling into a lab coat as he rushed through to the lab.

'Jesus, Penrose,' said Horace, 'give me a chance, it's only just arrived.'

'The signet ring is there, I understand.' Keith cautiously approached the hand which Horace already had laid out before him.

'Crossed swords,' said Horace, 'as the poor wee girl suggested. It certainly looks like the missing hand. I'll have to check it with the other and of course run tests but I think you can assume we have a matching pair.'

'And the dental records?' Keith asked.

'Nearly there, another hour or two, we'll certainly have the results tonight.'

'And do you have any early indications?'

'Not that I'm prepared to discuss with you, Penrose.'

Jack Curnow and Keith Penrose sat in an apparently unmoving queue on the Truro ring road in a vain attempt to get back to the station.

'So it's him then, isn't it?' said Jack. 'There can't be any way out of it, the signet ring is the real clincher.'

'I'm not going to say anything to Ellie until we have the results of the dental records,' Keith insisted.

'No, of course not, sir, but the fact is we now know the man is Simon Carter, don't we, it can't be anyone else.'

'Yes, I'm afraid we do,' said Keith, 'and that being the case we also know he is not Ellie's biological father.'

It was just after eight when Felicity heard from Keith Penrose again. Keith had stayed on in the office until Horace Greenaway had rung him with the news. He had then spent half an hour running and rerunning in his mind how best to break the news to

Ellie, whether to go over to St Ives, whether to telephone, whether to leave it until the morning .... In the end, telephoning Felicity seemed the best and only option.

'You have the results?' she said without preamble. 'Ellie is in bed so I can talk freely.'

'Yes I do,' said Keith, 'the body on the beach in Newquay is that of Simon Carter; his dental records match and if we needed further evidence, we have now found the missing hand. His watch has gone but his signet ring with the crossed swords is still on the hand we found and the hand matches the body.'

'And there is really no way there could be a mistake with the DNA match?'

'None at all, I'm afraid,' said Keith.

'So Ellie has to be told that her father isn't her father and that in any event he is dead.'

'Do you want me to come over and do it?' Keith said.

'No, no thanks,' said Felicity, 'I'll do it. I'll tell her in the morning.'

It was a clear starry night. Felicity went out onto the balcony and stood looking over the rooftops out towards the Bay. There was a theatrical moon hanging in the sky casting light over the water. It was quite beautiful.

'Oh Gilla,' Felicity whispered into the night sky, 'what have you done?'

17

'The awful thing is,' said Ellie, 'it didn't really come as a surprise. Somewhere deep in my subconscious or whatever you want to call it, I think I've always known that there was a distance between us, a lack of intimacy.'

It was four days since the news had been broken. Felicity and Ellie were having lunch in the Tate Gallery restaurant looking out over a stormy Porthmeor beach. Heavy clouds hung in the sky, huge seas pounded up the beach but there were no surfers, it was too choppy, too dangerous. It was their last meal out together in St Ives. The following day they were travelling up to Oxford. Simon's body had been released for burial and there was another funeral to organise. Felicity could not even begin to imagine how they were going to get through it.

'Are you sure that's the case,' said Felicity, 'or is it just that you spent most of your life apart from him so he was necessarily something of a shadowy figure in your childhood?'

'I used to beg Mum to tell me about my father – who he was, why he wasn't there, all that sort of stuff, and all the time she was lying.'

The flash of anger pleased Felicity, anything that would shake Ellie out of this terrible emotionless state. Even when she had been told the news there were no tears, just an apparent calm acceptance.

'I suppose it's possible,' said Fizzy, 'that she truly believed Simon was your father.'

'I know Mother was promiscuous, God knows there were plenty of "uncles" during my childhood, but you'd think she would have at least worked out who fathered her child, her only child,' Ellie said bitterly.

Felicity opened her mouth to protest and then shut it again. Ellie was right, of course.

'And you promise me you really have no idea who he is?' Ellie said.

Felicity shook her head. 'Until Simon found your mother – well, being unfaithful to him, I assumed the marriage was a good one. It was a busy period in my life; the children were still young but I was back working again, Charlie had a hectic law practice and the children's social life was fairly mad. It's one of the things I regret actually; I think during that period when you were tiny but your parents were still married, I rather neglected Gilla. Once Simon had gone and she was a single parent I did rally round but in your early babyhood I just assumed Simon was giving her the support she needed. When she was unfaithful to Simon, I was very cross with her at the time but in retrospect I can see that she was very lonely; Simon was working all the time, hardly ever at home, and she was such a people person, your Mum. I know Simon came to believe that what happened was as much his fault as your mother's.'

'Pretty generous of him in the circumstances,' Ellie said.

'Ellie, don't let this make you feel bitter.'

'Why not?' Ellie retorted. 'My mother is dead and the truth about who my father is has died with her. If *you* don't know who my father is, no one will ever know. If she didn't confide in you, she'd have confided in nobody – assuming of course she even knew. She was such a slag; there were probably half a dozen men it could be.'

'Ellie, stop it, you know that isn't true.'

'Isn't it? And think what a dreadful thing it was to do to Simon, palm him off with the belief that he had a daughter – think of all the years he supported me through school, through university, believing I was his daughter when I could be anyone's.'

'You were his daughter,' Felicity said quietly.

'Fizzy, we were related in no way. Our relationship was founded on a pack of lies,' Ellie bit back.

'Ellie, for once the truth doesn't matter. Simon died believing that he had a daughter – you. He was immensely proud of you and of your achievements. He was not a man who found it easy to communicate with people on an emotional level – I think that's why he was attracted to your mother because she was so outgoing, she forced him out of his shell – but just because he didn't tell you every five minutes that he loved you, never doubt that he did. He loved you and was proud to be your father and I know without a shadow of doubt that he would not have wanted it any other way.'

And there, at last, in the middle of the restaurant, Ellie began to cry.

Another funeral – this time the weather was awful, rain fell out of the sky all day. The trees around the churchyard had mostly shed their leaves, it was dank and cold, a vicious little wind tugged at people's coats and made them shiver. The same cast was present, the same vicar said much the same words, there was the same miserable trip to the crematorium which would ultimately result in the second casket to stand beside Gilla's which at the moment had been put on Simon's chest of drawers. There was an unreality about it – the destruction of a family in the matter of a few months.

This time though, there was a wake – not at the house (Ellie couldn't face that), but at the Old Parsonage Inn on the Woodstock Road, just a stone's throw from where Charlie Paradise had died. Ellie was in control, a natural hostess, any trace of the girl had long gone, she was now a young woman. Felicity was immensely proud of her. Keith Penrose had travelled up from Cornwall to be present at the funeral but Felicity had little time to talk to him. She longed to do so, feeling the need for his strength and reassurance, just to be around him would have made her feel better. She noticed him across the room having a long talk to Josh Buchanan and then realised that Josh was probably the only person present who he knew. When at last she had time to look for him, he had gone. She wondered if he was travelling back to Cornwall that night, or whether he was staying in Oxford. He had been oddly distant since Simon's body had been formally identified. He was always on the end of a phone if Ellie or she needed to clarify anything. He had reassured them that the hearing into Simon's death would return an open verdict – there would be no suggestion that Simon had committed suicide and certainly no evidence for it. However, he seemed to have distanced himself from her in some way. Felicity had hoped that Hugh Randall would be at the funeral, as he had been for Gilla's. She had fantasised about Keith confronting him, but there was no sign of Hugh.

At last all the guests left. A number of Ellie's friends had come down from Edinburgh to support her at the funeral and they were anxious to take her out for a drink. 'Are you sure you don't mind, Fizzy?' Ellie asked. She looked more animated than she had done in weeks, back amongst her own age group, among good friends. It was just what she needed.

'Please,' said Fizzy, 'go, and don't rush back. Have a good evening, I'll be fine.'

With the cheque Ellie had given her, Felicity paid the bill and collected her handbag from the little conference room where the wake had been held. It was evening now, people were arriving for dinner or drinks and she suddenly felt terribly alone. All her life since she had been a girl, if ever she had been at a loose end in Oxford she would ring Gilla. As she walked down the road towards her car, she thought of Keith. Where was he? The temptation to phone his mobile was almost irresistible, but she knew she must not. If there was any possibility that he was still in Oxford, to telephone him would be fatal. They would meet, they were alone in the city hundreds of miles from Cornwall, she was miserable and needed comforting – it was just too dangerous.

Half a mile up the Woodstock Road at the Cotswold Lodge Hotel, Keith was nursing a whisky in the bar. He could feel the weight of his mobile phone in his jacket pocket and the temptation to ring her was almost irresistible. Ellie would need her tonight; to try to lure her away from her responsibilities was quite wrong. He knew from the address that the Carters' house was very close by. He could go round;

see if they were all right – after all he had hardly spoken to Felicity at the wake. It was a bad idea – there would be other people there; Simon and Gilla and the Paradises were both Oxford families with masses of friends. He was sure he wasn't needed tonight.

Felicity staggered downstairs the following morning, heavy-eyed from lack of sleep. She found Ellie already bustling around in the kitchen looking better than she had in weeks.

'Goodness,' said Felicity, 'I am impressed. What time did you get in last night?'

'Oh not very late, about oneish. Did I wake you?'

'I don't know,' said Felicity, 'I was awake on and off all night, but I don't think I heard you come in.'

'Are you alright, Fizzy you look a bit …'

'Knackered?' Felicity suggested.

'Yes,' Ellie smiled, 'this must have been such an awful strain for you and you've been such a marvellous support.' She came up and put her arms around Felicity and gave her a hug. 'Thank you so much for everything.'

'Heavens,' said Felicity, 'that sounds rather conclusive. Are you going somewhere?'

'I've made plans, lots of them,' said Ellie, 'I'll make you a coffee and then we'll sit down and I'll tell you all about them.'

'So,' said Felicity moments later, 'spill the beans.'

233

'I'm going to go back to university now, today, if that's alright with you – and can get a lift – and over Christmas I'm going skiing with some friends. I've got to do something very positive this Christmas otherwise it's going to be awful. Also I'm going to sell this house and buy a flat in Edinburgh and I wondered if my home from home could be Cornwall with you.'

Felicity put out a hand and squeezed hers. 'My goodness, that's a lot of decisions, and yes, of course, my home is your home, that's a given. The only people who have ever really stayed in my spare room have been your mother, your father and Mel before she had her home in Cornwall – so now it's yours. Are you sure you want to make your home Edinburgh, though?'

'I think so,' said Ellie, 'I want to go on studying. If I get a good enough degree, I'd ultimately like to do a PhD. I love the city, I love the people, I have lots of friends up there. I've just got to work really hard now to make sure I get my First.'

'You'll get there, Ellie,' said Felicity.

'So do you think it's a good idea, all these plans?'

'I think it's marvellous.'

Ellie's face suddenly clouded. 'There is one thing.'

'What?' asked Felicity.

'Well, it's an enormous favour; in fact it's the biggest favour ever. I wondered if … well, not now but perhaps after Christmas, you would clear the house for me. I spoke to Josh yesterday and he said the best thing to do would be to put the house on the market in the spring so there is plenty of time. He says I can store any bits and pieces I want at his house, but there is very little I want to keep. I just don't think I can bear to break up our home nor can I face going through their things but I don't want a stranger to do it either.'

'Consider it done,' said Fizzy, 'I think it's the very least I can do.'

'I'm going to go and pack,' said Ellie; she started towards the kitchen door and then stopped. 'Oh, I knew I had something to show you – Keith gave me this.' She leant forward pulling the chain that was around her neck from under her shirt collar. Threaded onto it was a ring, Simon's signet ring. 'He suggested that I should do this and it's a good idea. He gave me the ring at the funeral and he said why not put it on a chain around your neck and then you'll know it's there but you won't have to explain it to anyone if you don't want to.'

'What a good idea,' Felicity said.

'Yes, he also said that in his line of business he had met plenty of biological fathers who should never have had a child, who didn't deserve to be called dad, but that I'd had a good father and that the DNA results didn't matter a damn – and do you know what Fizzy, he's right.'

'Yes, he is,' said Felicity, a little wistfully.

'He's such a lovely person,' said Ellie, 'I wish he could be, well you know, the man in your life.'

Whether it was the wisdom of Keith's words or the fact that this was Gilla's daughter, Felicity found herself saying what she thought she would never admit to a living soul. 'Me too.'

Ellie leant forward and gave her a quick hug. 'Still, who needs men anyway?' she said.

'Quite right,' Felicity agreed, smiling at her.

'Won't be long, we've got time for lunch somewhere before I go.' She was out of the door and thundering up the stairs. The marvellous resilience of youth, Felicity thought.

She was on the M5 again, heading west, and she knew she should have a genuine sense of achievement and even a sense of emotional freedom. Ellie was back up in Edinburgh; the house was clean, tidy and shut up till after Christmas with June going in once a week for a check around. There had been a few tears when she and Ellie had parted, but they had been her own, not Ellie's. Ellie was all right, she had good friends and her life ahead of her. She would have her black moments but that was what having a godmother and, come to that, a godfather in Josh, was all about. She was young, she would mend.

As she turned off the M5 onto the A30, Felicity remembered a holiday she and Gilla had spent in Crete. Gilla's mother had died shortly before Gilla took her 'A' levels, after a long and torturous battle with cancer. Gilla had made a complete mess of her 'A' levels – when she wasn't in the exam room staring at a blank sheet of paper, she was in the Lamb and Flag drinking herself senseless. In a desperate attempt to break this self-destructive cycle, Gilla's father had paid for Felicity and Gilla to have a ten days' package holiday in Crete. They had done very little – swam, sunbathed, water-skied, drank moderately, read books and talked about their aspirations for the future. By the middle of the holiday, Gilla had a plan. Her mother had owned a cottage in the centre of Woodstock where she had lived before she married Gilla's father. In the intervening years rather than sell it, she had let it to holidaymakers, most of them Americans visiting Blenheim Palace. Gilla was not going to resit her 'A' levels, she decided, she was going to persuade her father to let her take over the cottage. She would open a shop – arts and crafts aimed at the tourists – and would live above it. They spent the second half of the holiday making plans – doing amateurish costings and working out the strategy for approaching Gilla's father. As they flew out of Heraklion on their way home, Gilla had been looking to the future. The past contained a terrible sadness that would always be with her, but her eyes fixed on the horizon ahead. Felicity realised that Ellie was at the same point. So why did she feel so gloomy?

* * *

She arrived home mid-afternoon. Harvey was beside himself with joy to be home again and she felt she owed it to him to do the rounds of the beaches before attempting anything else. The cottage seemed very empty and she realised it was weeks since she had lived alone. Simon's remaining things were still in the cupboard in the spare room and they would have to stay there, she couldn't face doing anything with them at the moment. She went to the Fore Street Deli and bought some food and on the way home, on an impulse, stopped off to see Annie who immediately produced a cup of tea and a sausage roll for a very appreciative Harvey.

'You spoil that dog,' said Felicity reprovingly.

'And I suppose you don't, my bird. You look peaky, what's up?'

'Nothing,' Felicity said, 'I'm fine.'

'You're certainly not,' Annie said, with confidence. 'How's Ellie?' Felicity filled her in with Ellie's plans. 'What a sensible child she is,' Annie said, 'you should take a leaf out of her book, go off somewhere, have a holiday.'

Felicity shook her head, sudden tears pricking her eyes. 'I've nobody to go on holiday with, Annie, and I'd hate to go alone.'

'Then spend some time with those grandchildren of yours and stop feeling sorry for yourself. It's just self-indulgence – you may have lost your friends but you're still alive and kicking. Go to it, girl, it's what they would want, not you moping about.'

Felicity left Annie's with a smile. A good kick was what she had needed and Annie was right of course. She let herself into the cottage and was just unclipping Harvey's lead when she heard the phone ringing. She ran up the stairs – it was Josh.

'Just ringing to see you've arrived safely,' he said.

'That's kind,' said Felicity.

'I've been thinking,' he said, 'I've been working on Gilla and Simon's estate, which is complicated with them dying so close together – probate is going to take a while.'

'I imagine it is,' said Felicity.

'And then there is the house.'

'We're taking your advice and not attempting to sell that until the spring,' Felicity said, 'and first I've got to tackle the grisly task of clearing it.'

'When are you doing that?' Josh asked.

'After Christmas.'

'Alone?'

'Ellie can't face it and I don't blame her.'

'I'll help you if you want,' said Josh, 'I don't like the idea of you trying to tackle that on your own.'

'I'll remember that, thanks Josh.'

'Anyway,' said Josh, 'Ellie rang me this morning and told me of her plans to buy a flat in Edinburgh. Given what she's been through, I think she needs to get on with it.'

'I agree,' said Felicity.

'Being a confirmed old bachelor, I have some funds hanging around not doing anything so I wondered whether it might be a good idea if she used the money to put a deposit on the flat and then she can pay me back when the house is sold.'

'That's extraordinarily kind of you, Josh,' said Felicity, 'I think that's an excellent idea.'

'So would you ask her if she'd like to do that?' Josh said.

'No,' Felicity said, 'you talk to her about it. It's your idea, your kindness and she needs a father figure right now.'

Felicity spent the next couple of days with Mel. It was lovely being with the children but she still felt oddly restless.

'It's because there's no closure,' said Mel, picking up on her mother's feelings. 'Why don't you ring Keith Penrose and see if there have been any developments on the case?'

'I might just do that,' Felicity said.

She rang Keith the following morning and he sounded delighted to hear from her.

'I've been wondering when to ring you,' he said. 'You're back in Cornwall?'

'Yes.'

'And Ellie?'

'In Edinburgh, she seems to be fine. Keith, that was so kind of you, bringing her the ring, she really appreciated it.'

'I hope I got that right,' said Keith.

'You got it marvellously right. Keith, I was wondering if there was any chance of seeing you, I just want to understand what, if anything, is going to happen now …' her voice tailed away.

'Yes, of course. How are you fixed tomorrow night?'

'Nothing on,' said Felicity.

'I have a night off tomorrow. Barbara is at some Council meeting and Will has rugby training. Shall I come over to you?'

'I can come to Truro if you'd rather, if you're busy.'

'I think you've probably done enough driving around,' said Keith. 'Sloop at seven?'

'Perfect,' said Felicity, 'see you there.'

They bought drinks and settled themselves in a corner table.

'You look tired,' said Keith.

'Oh God,' said Felicity, 'in the over fifties, that's the euphemism for saying you look old.'

'On the contrary,' said Keith, gallantly, 'you look extremely young for your age Mrs Paradise, but tired.'

'You, on the other hand,' said Felicity, 'look absolutely fine.' And he did. This man who meant so much to her seemed to be able to raise her spirits as no one else could. She could feel the energy and enthusiasm that flowed from him.

'I am feeling quite pleased with myself at the moment,' said Keith, 'we've had a particularly tricky unsolved murder that has been on the books for some months – in Bodmin – drug-related, of course. Anyway, we cracked it a couple of days ago, the villain is behind bars and we've got enough evidence to put him away, very satisfactory.'

'Well done,' said Felicity, raising her glass to him, 'what a good policeman you are.'

'I think I sense something slightly patronising in that remark.'

'Absolutely not,' said Felicity, 'but as we're talking police business, I suppose you've got no further with finding out what happened with Simon?'

Keith instantly sobered. 'I'm really sorry,' he said, 'but I don't think we are going anywhere with Simon Carter's death. I had a meeting with the Super the day after the funeral and he has essentially told me to drop it.'

'So he thinks Simon killed himself?' Felicity asked.

'No, I don't necessarily think he does, but the death is unexplained and we have not a thread of evidence to suggest it was foul play.'

'So the death of Alex Button and the incident with the speedboat don't amount to anything?'

'The accident with the speedboat could have been just that, Felicity, an accident.'

'And his house being broken into?'

'Local villains in the area would have probably known there had been a death in the family and that the house was empty.'

'He wouldn't have walked out on us, Keith.'

'I know that,' said Keith, 'you know that, but how to prove it. There are no witnesses, there was no sign of any scuffle or forced entry into your cottage. He could have gone walking somewhere, slipped and fallen into the sea.' Keith reached across and took her hand. 'I think you're going to have to face up to the fact that you're never going to know how Simon died and neither is Ellie.'

'If only I could see it,' Felicity said.

'How do you mean?' Keith asked.

'You know my second sight or whatever you like to call it? Gilla used to call it "Fizzy's Funny Moments".'

Keith squeezed her hand and let go of it. He took a sip of his wine and gazed at her over the rim of his glass. 'Have you tried to think yourself into imagining what happened to Simon, is there any way you can trigger it?'

'None at all,' said Felicity, 'and I'm starting to think maybe I've lost the ability.'

'When were you first aware you could see things other people couldn't?' Keith asked.

Felicity shrugged. 'I don't know, about five I think. My grandmother on my mother's side was the same, so my mother wasn't surprised, she just accepted it as something normal and so did I. It's never been much help, actually – I've never been able to see the answers to exams or know the correct numbers for the National Lottery. Most of what I see is just shadows and feelings – the clearest image I've ever had was when Charlie died, but then I suppose that's not surprising given that he was my husband.'

'I'm sorry there is nothing more we can do about Simon,' Keith said, 'but if anything should come to you, or you come across anything we could use as evidence, you know I'll take it up again, whatever my Super says.'

'Thanks Keith,' said Felicity.

'There was something I was going to talk to you about,' Keith said, 'how many people have you told about the lack of DNA match between Simon and Ellie?'

'Nobody at all,' said Felicity, 'Ellie and I talked about it and we decided that apart from the police and presumably your forensic man, no one would know. We both felt we owed it to Gilla to keep her secret quiet and also to Simon – above all to Simon – because he died believing he was Ellie's father. Ellie told me what you said to her at the funeral. It was a very sensitive and sensible thing to say and she has really taken it on board. I don't think she is particularly curious about trying to find her biological father, maybe later – you know those sort of emotional triggers, like when she has a baby of her own or something …' her voice tailed away. 'Why do you ask, Keith?'

'So Josh Buchanan, who I understand is also a godparent to Ellie, knows nothing about the DNA mismatch?'

'No, not from either Ellie or I, not unless you told him. I saw you talking to him at the funeral.'

'No, I didn't tell him. I will never tell anybody, it would be most unprofessional. The DNA testing is a confidential matter.'

Felicity frowned. 'So why the questions then, Keith?'

'Josh had drunk too much at the wake, I don't know whether you realised that?'

Felicity shook her head. 'No, I barely saw him to be honest.'

'He was telling me how much the family had meant to him, both Ellie's family and yours, how much you all meant to him and how he had no family of his own but you. He was a bit of a bore, poor chap, but I knew no one else apart from you and Ellie and I was only at the funeral as a matter of courtesy – not in an official capacity.'

'It was kind of you to come,' Felicity said.

'No, not at all.' He hesitated a moment. 'Were you aware that Josh had an affair with your friend Gilla?'

'No,' said Felicity, 'I'm sure you're wrong there.'

245

'Not according to Josh. He said it had happened when they were both lonely. His marriage – I hadn't realised he'd been married – had broken up and Gilla was married to Simon but Simon was never there, he was always working.'

'I honestly didn't know,' said Felicity, 'but I feel sure I would have known – Gilla and I told each other everything.'

'Well maybe it was wishful thinking, on his part, brought on by the drink, I don't know. I don't really know him and I certainly didn't know Gilla.' He hesitated. 'But I do know Ellie and I like her enormously. If Josh Buchanan was having an affair with her mother during the time she was married to Simon then it is possible that Josh is Ellie's father.'

'Did he say that they had the affair before Ellie was born?'

'No, he didn't,' said Keith. 'I was anxious not to appear too curious.'

'I suppose it is possible,' said Felicity. 'I just can't understand why Charlie or I wouldn't have spotted it.'

'They would have been very discreet, wouldn't they?' Keith said. 'After all Gilla was still married.'

Felicity shook her head as if trying to clear it. 'They certainly spent a lot of time together but it was always with us.'

'Was it?' Keith said, smiling.

'Well I thought so, but maybe not.'

'I know you've had your doubts about Josh Buchanan. How would you feel about it if he was Ellie's father?'

'I think he is probably just about ready for fatherhood, he's certainly nearly grown up, at last.' said Felicity.

'And would he be any good at it?' Keith asked.

'Do you know, I rather think he would.'

'So are you going to talk to him about it?'

'I don't know,' said Felicity, 'I'll need to think. Certainly, the starting point would be to talk to Josh. There is no point in telling Ellie unless there is a serious possibility that Josh is her father.'

'If your chum Gilla was married and having an affair with Josh Buchanan, I'd have hardly thought there would be a third man involved.'

'I'd like to think not,' Felicity replied.

18

Having always been cursed with an impulsive nature, on leaving Keith that night Felicity's instincts were to ring Josh straight away. On reaching home though, it occurred to her that sleeping on such a potentially momentous piece of news was probably a good thing. By morning, she was beginning to question the wisdom of telling anyone anything just yet. It was a huge responsibility to keep Keith's suspicions to herself, but as the day wore on, she became increasingly sure that it was the right thing to do. Josh and Ellie were already forming a closer relationship than they had ever had before, caused by the winding up of her parents' estate, and then there was his very generous offer to allow her to buy herself a flat with his money until hers was available. It would be good to let their relationship develop naturally without the pressure of this possible forced intimacy. There was, of course, the distinct possibility that they would work things out for themselves. Ellie only had to confide in Josh that Simon was not her biological father for the penny to drop. Somehow, though, Felicity thought that this was unlikely. Ellie was a very private person and although Josh was her godfather, Felicity doubted she would confide in him. As Simon had always believed Ellie to be his daughter, then Felicity suspected that Ellie would consider it disloyal to share the knowledge that she was not with anyone else. Felicity was tempted to telephone Keith and run her decision past him; then she gave herself a severe talking-to – she must not encourage this dependence on Keith. It was a simple decision really. She was going up to Oxford in January to clear the house and she was bound to see plenty of Josh then. That would be time enough to discuss Ellie's parentage. Ellie had endured enough shocks in the last few months to last most people a lifetime. This one would keep.

The weeks leading up to Christmas were very busy. Mel had started back at work two mornings a week and although it was recognised that now she had two children, she ultimately would need a childminder, on an short-term basis Felicity was happy to help out and cover while Mel was at work. James and his family came down to stay for a few days before Christmas and with the house awash with children, there was no time to think of anything much but the next meal and the logistics of getting through the day. It was just what she needed. Now and again she would glance at the financial press or hear something on the radio; Carlyon had stabilized,

249

the Bank was expected to make losses in its first year but would move swiftly into profit according to the Chairman, Hugh Randall. She heard nothing from Keith and made no attempt to contact him. Shortly before Christmas she received a card from him, wishing her a Happy Christmas but she could not respond in kind – it would have looked odd.

The streets of St Ives, having cleared after the October half term, remained quiet in the build-up to Christmas. It was now possible to walk down Fore Street and know pretty much everyone you passed. She loved the town when it was like this and felt a real part of the community; it was balm to the wounds created by the loss of Gilla and Simon. Ellie seemed to be doing well and working hard. She flew out to France on the day before Christmas Eve with a group of friends, and from the shouted greeting at Heathrow before the flight took off, she sounded in good form. Charlie's first Christmas was a delight, not because he knew what was going on, but because Minty did. The whole ritual of a child's Christmas: Christingle, the stockings, the stories, made Felicity feel very nostalgic for the time when her own children were young. What a precious time it had been, but of course you never realise just how precious it is at the time, she thought.

The town filled up for the New Year

celebrations, always a big event in St Ives. Mel and Martin suggested she spent New Year's Eve with them but she thought they needed time alone and so she decided to see the New Year in alone this time. She had been invited to several parties but none of them appealed. It had been an awful year and while it was good to see an end to it, she couldn't link its passing with any kind of celebration – it just didn't feel right. She decided to treat herself to some smoked salmon and half a bottle of champagne. Fancy dress was the St Ives tradition for the evening ahead, that and copious quantities of alcohol. In Johns the Off Licence, she found herself buying her champagne alongside a very drunk fairy, a member of the French Foreign Legion and an octopus – it was definitely time to go home.

Wrapped up in a coat she sat out on her balcony with her glass of champagne watching the fireworks and seeing in the New Year. Harvey hated fireworks and had taken himself downstairs to her bedroom, so she was quite alone. During the course of the evening her thoughts rarely strayed from Gilla and Simon.

'Where are you Gilla?' she whispered into the night sky, but there was no sense of her friend being close. She had simply gone.

As the clock struck midnight, she first raised her glass to Ellie. Good luck with the rest of your life, darling Ellie, she thought and then her thoughts turned to Keith. She knew they were distancing themselves from one another and she knew it was right but it still hurt so much. She wondered what he was doing and raised her glass again.

'Happy New Year, Keith,' she said aloud into the night.

Keith Penrose couldn't stand New Year's Eve parties, the false jollity, the anticipation of midnight which always turned out to be an anti-climax; the drinking for drinking's sake rather than for pleasure. When he and Barbara had first married, he had extracted a promise from her that they would never go to New Year's Eve parties and when the children were small, it was, in any case, impractical. In the last few years however, Barbara had dragged him along to the parties of several of her colleagues at work and tonight was no exception. The party was at a rather grand house on the water's edge in Malpas. It belonged to a very pompous councillor who made a great many jokes at Keith's expense about the long arm of the law keeping the party in order. It was very tedious. A taxi was coming to pick them up at 12.30 and by nine o'clock in the evening, Keith had wondered how on earth he would last that long, his face aching from forced smiles. At last midnight came and he managed to separate himself from the baying crowd and slip out into the hosts' garden, which he had to admit was beautiful. He raised his glass in silent toast to Felicity. Let's hope 2009 is a better year for you, he thought –

it could hardly be worse.

In the second week of January, Felicity and Harvey left for Oxford. The gardens were very quiet and so Martin was able to care for his children while Mel was working. Felicity reckoned she would need at least ten days, maybe longer, to sort out the house. It was going to be a grisly business. She had extracted from Ellie a list of things she would like to keep and Josh had already cleared the papers from Simon's study. They had decided it was better to leave the house furnished until it was sold, so it was really just a question of clearing away personal effects. Gilla and Simon had lived in the house since before Ellie was born and Gilla was not noted for her tidiness – it was a huge undertaking involving sacks of rubbish and endless visits to charity shops. The days slipped by and she finished each one dusty, stiff and exhausted. Harvey hated the whole thing and spent most of the time under the bed in the spare room where Felicity was sleeping. She had intended to see some old friends in the evenings but somehow she couldn't face it. Josh had invited her out to dinner on a couple of occasions, but she had declined, she hadn't the energy.

The room she had been dreading was Gilla and Simon's bedroom, it was too intimate and so full of Gilla. In the top drawer of Gilla's chest of drawers there was a little box containing special mementos;

there was a picture of her mother and father, of her and her mother, a prayer book she had been given on her confirmation and a handmade birthday card with a picture of Gilla and Felicity on the front and inscribed in a childish hand – *Happy 10th Birthday Gilla, double figures! Lots of Love Fizzy. XX*

Felicity sat on the edge of the bed for some while, moved beyond tears that Gilla should have kept this card all these years. She carefully slipped it back in the envelope and put it back in her own handbag. The memories kept on crowding in, she felt like she was drowning in them.

It was during what she hoped would be the last afternoon of clearing that Felicity found the letter. It was in Gilla's dressing table drawer. It was addressed to Felicity Paradise, but the hand she recognised, was that of Simon.

Dearest Fizzy,

I have tried to be logical about this. If anything should happen to me I know you would not let Ellie clear her mother's things alone, and I am assuming, therefore, that you will find this letter.

I am going to try and make a life for myself without Gilla, I really will try but it is going to be hard going, for I see no future without her. There is Ellie, of course, but this is what I wanted to tell you. Fizzy, Ellie is not my daughter. Gilla and I knew before we married that I would

254

not be able to father children. Gilla, being Gilla, delicately described it as me firing blanks, my sperm count is non-existent apparently. When Gilla became pregnant she expected me to leave her, but I loved her so much I was happy to take on the child, but insisted that I should not know the name of the father, I couldn't bear to know. She respected that request, did not tell me then and has never since and so now, of course, I will never know. It is why I reacted so violently when I stumbled on the affair Gilla was having when Ellie was a baby. She admitted that the man in question was not Ellie's father and two infidelities were too much for me, which is why I took myself off to Hong Kong. If anything should happen to me, Fizzy, Ellie has a substitute mother in you, but I think it would be good for her to know who her real father is. Gilla took her secret to her grave, I don't want to do the same thing so help her find her father, Fizzy, if such a situation should arise.

All my love and thank you for the support you have given and continue to give to my family.

Simon.

Felicity read the letter several times and then reaching for her mobile she telephoned Josh. 'How about dinner tonight?' she said.

'Done, I'll pick you up at seven-thirty.'

'At last,' said Josh, as Felicity opened the front door, 'you've been very reclusive since you've been here.'

'I know, I'm sorry,' said Felicity, 'it's just been such an all-consuming task.'

'Exactly, so you should have let me help,' said Josh.

'Probably,' said Felicity, 'but it was just something I felt I had to do alone.'

'I've booked a table at the Lemon Tree.'

Felicity's face fell. 'It's awfully noisy there, Josh. Can't we go somewhere quieter where we can talk?'

They ended up at The Feathers in Woodstock. 'I used to meet Gilla for lunch here sometimes,' Josh said, when they had ordered their wine and food. It gave Felicity the perfect introduction.

'I have a letter here,' she said, 'from Simon, which I think you should read.' She handed the letter over and watched Josh's face as he absorbed its contents. His handsome face creased into a frown, his slightly florid complexion paled. 'You're Ellie's father, aren't you Josh?' Felicity said quietly. The wine arrived and they did not speak until the waiter had left.

'I suppose I could be,' Josh stammered. 'But Ellie mustn't ever know about this – after all she's been through. We mustn't tell her, Fizzy.'

'She already knows Simon isn't her father,' Felicity said.

'How?' said Josh, his face now bleached with shock.

'Simon was identified first by DNA and then by

dental records. Naturally his DNA was compared with Ellie's and found not to be a match. At that point it could have been assumed that the body wasn't that of Simon Carter but Keith Penrose had this feeling it was, and so pursued the dental records rather than start comparing the DNA with other missing people. It was just a hunch but he was proved to be right, then ...' she hesitated, 'then Simon's hand was found with the signet ring and that was that.'

'So Ellie knows that Simon isn't her father and so does Keith Penrose?' Felicity nodded. 'But why has neither of them said anything? I had a long talk to Keith at the funeral.'

'In Keith's case,' said Felicity, 'it wasn't his secret to tell. In Ellie's, I think she had decided that since Simon believed himself to be her father, it would be disloyal to start looking for a biological father when Simon had so brilliantly fulfilled the role.'

'But Simon did know that he wasn't Ellie's father.'

'Yes,' said Felicity patiently, 'but Ellie doesn't know that and I only learnt about it this afternoon. I found this letter in Gilla's dressing table drawer.'

'Do you think it's a suicide letter?'

'I don't think so,' said Felicity, 'I'm not sure what it is. It's all about Ellie rather than himself, it's hard to tell what was in his mind. I expect he wrote it shortly after Gilla's death, but it's undated so we've no real idea – he was in such a terrible state around that time.'

'Gilla and I had a brief fling when I was up at Cambridge,' said Josh after a pause, 'she had her shop by then and I was reading Law. I had this very unreliable girlfriend and just before the Clare College May ball, she ditched me. I had the tickets for the ball and I didn't want to be seen without a partner so I asked Gilla. She came, dazzled everyone of course. I was very proud of her and one thing led to another and we ended up in bed.'

'But that was years before Ellie was born.'

'Yes,' said Josh, 'but it sort of established a pattern. If either of us were unlucky in love we would end up together for a while.'

'I had absolutely no idea,' said Felicity.

'Good,' said Josh.

'But why did you keep it from me? I feel a slightly hurt that neither of you could confide in me.'

'We knew you wouldn't approve. First, last and always Gilla and I were friends, it was just sometimes we were lovers too. You've always been a bit of a prude, Fizzy.'

Felicity smiled at him. 'I suppose I have,' she said, thinking of Keith.

'Anyway the years went by,' said Josh, 'and Gilla married and as far as I was concerned, that was the end of that. But after a year or so it was clear she was finding life with Simon pretty dull, not because she didn't care about him, she did, but because he was never there, he was always working. He went off to some banking conference in New York and we went to the Lake District for an extremely sexy weekend. We spent most of it in bed, we drank far too much and it did us both a power of good. I think it could have been the weekend that Ellie was conceived.'

'So what happened next?' Felicity asked.

'Gilla told us all, if you remember, at Norham Gardens one evening. You and Charlie had us both to supper, as usual, and she announced during the meal that she and Simon were expecting a baby. I have to say it never entered my head that it could be mine, I simply saw that weekend in isolation as one of our dalliances and of no consequence. It never occurred to me that she would be careless and I just didn't "do the maths" as they say.'

'And did you continue to sleep with her after Ellie was born?' Felicity could not keep the criticism out of her voice.

'No, we never slept together again. It wasn't me who Simon found in bed with her, and caused the breakup of their marriage. I don't know who it was, some random bloke, but not me. Somehow, once she was a mother, I couldn't somehow.'

'Not even when the marriage broke up?'

Josh shook his head. 'By then we had moved on to a different sort of relationship and we deliberately never met alone. I handled all her legal work but we always met in my office and other than that, socially, we only ever met at your house, or occasionally at a restaurant for lunch. She was still married, you see, and Ellie being the child of that marriage, I somehow felt it was wrong to put a further wedge between husband and wife, even though they had parted.' He paused and sipped his wine, then looked down at his plate. The suave, sophisticated Josh had gone, he looked suddenly vulnerable.

'There is something you're not telling me,' Felicity said.

Josh took a deep breath and raised his eyes to meet Felicity's. 'I loved her, you see, so very much. There have always been plenty of women in my life, you know that, but Gilla is the only one I loved. It's ironic. I knew she was still very fond of Simon and showed no inclination to want to divorce him and since I believed he was Ellie's father, I stayed my hand. The truth is that when Simon left I would have married Gilla if I could, but I didn't want to destroy the possibility of Ellie having her mother and father back together again.'

Felicity reached over and squeezed Josh's hand. 'A bit of a tangled web and what a waste, all those years. I'm sorry, Josh. I suppose it's possible Ellie could be someone else's? Gilla was a naughty girl,' she suggested.

'It's possible but I doubt it. At that stage she still really wanted to make the marriage work. Being unfaithful to him with me was safe; she knew I'd never cause trouble. I think Ellie is mine, Fizzy, I really do.'

'So what do we do?' Felicity asked.

'We tell Ellie, I suppose.'

Ellie arrived in Oxford two days later. The house was cleared and there was just a pile of things waiting in Simon's study which Felicity had identified as items Ellie would want to keep. The plan was that Ellie would give Felicity's selection final approval and then everything would be stored in Josh's house until Ellie had bought her own flat. So far as Ellie was concerned this was the sole reason for the visit.

Felicity met her at Oxford station. They had not seen each other since just after the funeral and Ellie looked great, still a little suntanned from skiing, slimmer and more confident.

The two women hugged. 'I hope it's not going to be too awful for you, coming back to the house.'

'No, I'm glad to do it,' said Ellie, 'I'd like to come back once more and say goodbye to the old place. If one was a psychiatrist, one would probably call it closure.'

Felicity smiled. 'One probably would.'

Felicity's pile of memorabilia was approved and one or two pieces of furniture and some pictures were added. Felicity had bought some food so that they could have supper in and she had agreed with Josh that it would be best if she broke the news to Ellie alone and then saw how Ellie wanted to play it.

Felicity put a casserole in the oven, poured them both a glass of wine and sat Ellie down at the kitchen table.

'Ellie, there is something I need to show you.' She handed Ellie Simon's letter. Ellie read it slowly and carefully. 'So he knew,' she said, looking up at Felicity, tears in her eyes, 'he knew all those years and yet he treated me just like a daughter.'

'You weren't just like a daughter,' said Felicity, 'you were his daughter.'

'He paid for my education, my school trips, everything and then when he came back to Mum he was marvellously supportive to me … and all the time he knew.'

'I think you need to look at this a different way,' said Felicity. 'You provided him with the only opportunity he would ever have to be a father – he provided you with the father but equally you provided him with a child.'

Ellie was silent for a few minutes, biting her lower lip. Felicity braced herself for the question that she knew was coming.

'So who is my father then, Fizzy?'

Felicity took a deep breath. 'Darling, I rather think it's Josh.'

Felicity left them to it as soon as Josh arrived. The moment Ellie knew the possibility that Josh was her father, she had asked whether he could come round. They greeted one another a little shyly and at that point Felicity had found a pressing engagement with her packing upstairs. She did not want to leave Oxford while she was still needed but she was hoping to return to Cornwall within a couple of days. The voices rumbled on downstairs and so, having slipped out of the front door to give Harvey his last walk of the night, she crept back upstairs, showered and went to bed. Ellie arrived in her bedroom an hour or so later, flushed and happy.

'Of all the people it could have been, thank God it's Josh! Mum had the most ghastly taste in men, except for Simon and Josh – to think it's Josh, what a relief,' she said throwing herself down on the end of Felicity's bed.

'Remember you don't know it's Josh for certain yet,' Felicity said, cautiously.

'No, but we're pretty sure. Josh has found out what we need to do. We're going to go to his GP in the morning to get a referral to the Churchill Hospital – they'll do a DNA and then we'll know for sure.'

'Don't get your hopes up too much, darling, in case we're all wrong.'

'You must think Mum was an awful slapper,' said Ellie, eyeing Felicity suspiciously.

Felicity smiled and shook her head. 'No, I just don't want to see you hurt anymore.'

'I'm fine, I'm sure Josh is my father, we've even got the same hands.'

'OK, off to bed with you and we'll get things

moving in the morning.'

Felicity could not sleep that night, she was restless; too hot one minute, too cold the next. At three o'clock in the morning she went downstairs and made herself a cup of tea. Climbing back up the stairs to the spare room, she paused for a moment outside Ellie's room and on impulse went inside. It was still essentially a little girl's room; there was a line of teddies on the window seat and a childish school desk where Ellie had studied so hard over the years. She walked over to the bed and gazed down on her goddaughter. Ellie was fast asleep; she looked very peaceful and heart-breakingly young. Suddenly Felicity was aware of a shadowy figure beside her, indistinct but infinitely recognizable. It was Gilla standing next to her, also looking down at the sleeping girl. The shadow didn't speak but in her head Felicity heard Gilla's distinct husky voice.

'Well done, old girl.'

EPILOGUE

January 2009, St Ives, Cornwall

A week after her return from Oxford, Felicity invited Chief Inspector Keith Penrose for a drink one evening. He accepted hesitantly and arrived looking awkward, kissing her briefly on the cheek and then striding out through the French windows onto the balcony, as if to put as much distance between them as possible. Felicity was hurt. She poured them wine, coaxed him in from the balcony where it was extremely cold, firmly shut the French windows and sat him down in a Windsor chair beside the Aga, placing herself in the other chair some distance from him. He was still jumpy. She handed him Simon's letter.

'I thought you'd like to see this,' she said.

He read it with great concentration. 'How do you see this?'

'Well, we all feel – Ellie, Josh and I – that it isn't

obviously a suicide note nor can you say that there's any definite sense of him believing his life was under threat – it's neither. It's totally inconclusive. As I see it, here is a man in the midst of a huge emotional crisis, but it's very unclear why he thinks I need to be privy to the secret, why he feels he shouldn't continue to carry it alone.'

Keith nodded. 'Maybe he wrote it to be ambiguous on purpose, worried that if it appeared to be a suicide note it would be very upsetting for everyone he cared about.'

'Maybe,' said Felicity, 'but he was in such a state at the time I don't think he would have been in the mood to play double bluff. I tend to think it's just what he said, the need to share this vital piece of information now that he was the only person left who knew the truth. If he'd planned to throw himself into the sea, he'd have known there was a good chance his DNA would be compared with Ellie's to establish identification.'

'You're assuming,' said Keith, 'that a man in his emotional state would be able to work out something like that. I think you're taking things a step too far. It seems to me he thought there was a possibility that he might not be around for much longer and that he wanted to share the truth of Ellie's fatherhood with you, but …' Keith hesitated, 'that sense of mortality could simply be the result of having seen his wife die so unexpectedly – well one minute, dead the next.'

266

Felicity nodded. 'I suppose the truth is, Keith, we're just never going to know, are we?'

Keith shook his head. 'No, I'm afraid we're not.'

'I do have some good news, though. They ran another DNA test and Josh *is* Ellie's father. They're both delighted – so you see, Chief Inspector, you were right again.'

Her words were greeted with barely a smile.

'You're being very odd tonight,' Felicity said.

'Am I?' Keith took a sip of his wine, holding his glass like a lifeline. Felicity studied him in silence for a moment.

'You've come to say goodbye, haven't you?' she said in a small voice.

He put down his glass and crossed the space between them, lifted her out of the chair by her shoulders, wrapped his arms around her and kissed her as if his life depended on it. The misery and loneliness of the last months evaporated in his arms, but even as she returned his kisses she knew that this was not the beginning of a new relationship but the end of an old one.

At last they drew apart a little and she rested her head on his shoulder. 'It's OK,' she whispered, 'you don't have to explain anything, I understand completely.' His embrace tightened around her.

'I can't bear this,' he said, 'but I just see no other way. I can't give you the love and support you richly deserve. Dear God, I'm only flesh and blood, I want to

267

make love to you and be with you forever, but I can't, mustn't. I love you so much.'

Felicity raised her head and looked deep into his eyes. 'It's OK, Keith, I agree with you, you're right. We need to end this.'

'And I'm such a terrible liar; I've always been since a boy. Barbara can see straight through me, I would never be able to carry it off.'

Felicity stroked his cheek tenderly. 'I know my love, I know. It's alright, everything is alright.'

'But it isn't, is it?' said Keith.

'It's enough that I know you love me,' Felicity said.

'And always will,' Keith said, 'always for the rest of my life you will be in my thoughts.'

'Are you expecting us never to see each other again?' said Felicity. There was a note of panic in her voice and he picked it up immediately.

'No, no, of course not, but we need to put some distance between us – we mustn't put ourselves in this sort of situation again.'

Felicity stared at him. 'What situation?'

'Alone, in the house, with you now – the thought of tearing myself away from you at this moment – it's a bloody nightmare.'

'Well then, Chief Inspector, we'd better put an end to your nightmare. Come on, I'll walk up to your car with you. It's in Barnoon, right?' She freed herself from his embrace and lifted the door key off its hook by the Aga.

'I want to say more,' he said helplessly.

'What more do you want to say?' Felicity asked gently.

Keith shrugged. 'That no one in my life has ever meant as much to me as you do, that ...'

'Stop,' said Felicity. 'We love each other and will always do so. Let's not agonise, let's just take comfort from that. Come on.'

They walked slowly hand in hand up to the car park. At his car they paused.

'Well Chief Inspector, you didn't get your man this time, did you?' said Felicity, with a smile.

'No need to rub it in, Mrs Paradise. You can't win them all, not in my line of work.'

'No, I suppose not.'

'I might not have solved the case, but I did prove one thing though.' He was smiling at her and it broke her heart. She wanted to take him in her arms and never let go.

'What?' she asked, with effort.

'I've proved that what the public at large tend to believe these days is probably right.'

'Which is?'

'That banks and bankers do get away with murder.'